# When the *Heart* Turns

# Cold 3

# BLACK ICE:

## *THE FAMILY BLOODLINE*

*Book 3 in the Lacy Ice Series*

## *by C.Y. Marshall*

## *previously writing as Charlotte*

+

Black Ice: The Family Bloodline is book four of the When the Heart Turns Cold series. Please read the previous books to have a better understanding of the characters and circumstances in Black Ice.
Thank You

# Chapter 1

Nala was perplexed as she walked to her car and got in. Her visit with Robert Randstad was as weird as the dreams she was having about him. She had no clue what his final words meant to her. It was almost as if he knew her personally and intimately. She didn't want him to get in her head, but he had. From their conversation, he had her spooked.

Nala turned on her phone. There were several missed calls and messages. At that time, nothing was of interest except her visit with Randstad. Nala started her car and drove off. She thought that Randstad would be strapped to a table being fed lethal injection for his final meal within a week. It would be then she would learn the mystery of the visit.

When Nala pulled into her driveway, it was close to 6 in the evening. She had stopped off on the way home and picked up a bottle of wine. Her night was going to be spent taking a hot bubble bath and drinking. She was surprised to see Kendrick's car parked in the driveway. She thought to herself that he was the last person she wanted to see. Why was he there? What could he possibly want?

Kendrick got out of the car and leaned against it as Nala parked. She was not in the mood to see him, so she knew she was going to get rid of him quickly. When she got out of the car, Kendrick looked her over like she was a piece of prime rib. She could hear him salivating over her, and she loved it.

"So, what do I owe the honor of your presence?" she asked sarcastically.

"I was hoping we could talk."

"Don't you believe in calling before you show up at someone's house?"

"I did call. You didn't answer."

"Well, that means I didn't want to talk to you or be bothered! Get it?" she asked as she walked over to the front door and unlocked it.

Nala turned around to Kendrick standing there like a lost puppy. She really hated the man he had become. In a million years, she would never have expected her soon-to-be ex-husband to have turned into a lying, cheating bitch.

"I'm not asking for much of your time, but the least you could do is hear what I have to say."

Nala gave him a surprised look and began to laugh. She couldn't believe the audacity of him thinking she owed him anything. She figured it was that male entitlement most men believe they deserve. But to be honest, he had her curious. What made him drive all the way to her house and wait for her until she arrived home? That sounded a little desperate to her. Although she was still whirling from her visit with Randstad, she figured she would hear what he had to say.

She moved to the side and gestured for him to enter the house. Kendrick walked in and stood at the door, looking around. His expression was that of a man who knew he fucked up but couldn't come back. Nala dropped her keys and pocketbook on the table by the front door and walked toward the kitchen.

Kendrick wasn't sure if he should follow, but he took a chance and did. Nala took a glass from the cabinet and took the wine out of the bag. She sat down at the kitchen table, opened it and filled her glass to the top. Kendrick's eyes wandered the kitchen as he tried not to look at her. She drank most of it and sat her glass down. Nala looked at him and waited for him to speak.

"How have you been?" he asked nervously, knowing the possible response he was going to get.

Nala gave him a smirk as she poured more wine into her glass. The sight of him was starting to make her feel disgusted. Maybe hearing what he had to say wasn't such a good idea. He was definitely interrupting the plans she had to take a nice, hot bubble bath and get drunk. She drank some of the wine and wiped it from her mouth as a little of it trickled down her chin. Nala sat the glass down hard and sighed loudly.

"No small talk, okay. What do you want?"

"Listen, I know things didn't work out for us. For what it's worth, I'm sorry about that. But things happen, and life goes on. Anyway, before you hear it from someone else, I wanted to tell you that Crystal is pregnant. Whatever tension or hatred you two have for each other needs to stop because she can't be stressed. Now, I know you hate me and her, but I know you wouldn't want anything to happen to an innocent baby because its mother is stressed. You're not like that. You're a good woman."

Nala felt a knot in her stomach begin to twist and tighten. She was good at hiding her expressions, so she knew her face didn't tell how she really felt. Truth be told, his news delivered a major blow to her. Nala thought back to the beginning of their relationship when they had talked about having children. One of the reasons they bought the home she still lives in was because of the space for having children and the school district. She thought back to how many children they spoke about having and the names they were going to be given. The news hurt her, but it also angered her. Nala became so angry inside she visualized stabbing him in his jugular vein and watching the blood squirt from his neck. She was so fixated on the image she hadn't heard him calling her name.

"Nala, did you hear me?"

"Yes, I did," she said, quickly regrouping. "I'm just trying to figure out why you felt the need to tell me any of this?"

"Look, I know you have been sneaking up on Crystal in dark spots trying to intimidate her, and I get it. But now, the stakes are much too high for that. She's pregnant."

"Who gives a fuck? You know you have a lot of nerve coming over here to tell me about your bitch being pregnant. You seem to think it's okay to come to my home and defend that hoe. You came here a few weeks ago, insinuating that I was stalking her and to stop. Now, you come here telling me she's pregnant like I give a flying fuck, and you think I'm supposed to care. Well, news flash, I don't. Now, this is how this is going to play out," Nala said, getting up and leaving the kitchen to walk to the front door.

Kendrick sighed and got up to follow her. She opened the front door, and Kendrick walked out, then turned around to face her.

"You've been pushing your luck with me. Coming over here like captain save a hoe and expecting me to care about you or that thing you're with. You don't want to keep pushing the envelope with me. You really don't want to see what I'm capable of doing to you if you keep fucking bothering me. So, I'm going to give you fair warning. Don't come here again with no bullshit about your girl, your unborn baby or whatever. Contrary to what you think, I'm like that, and I'm not a good woman. What you need to know is I don't care about you, Crystal, or your fucking kid. Now, I'm going to close my door, and if you feel the need to come here again, then I just might have to kill you!"

Nala slammed the door, almost hitting his face had he not quickly moved back. She went into the kitchen and got her wine, and then went into her office. She sat in front of her computer and turned it on. Nala was still digesting what Kendrick just told her.

*A baby,* she thought to herself as she pulled up her email. At times, everything seemed so surreal to her. Although their marriage wasn't perfect, even though it looked that way, they still made it work and loved each other. Nala's biggest mistake was befriending a hoe. She knew women could be scandalous and conniving, but she didn't see that in Crystal. She thought she saw a woman who she could call a friend. How funny is that since that same woman has her husband and is pregnant with his child? Whatever the case, Nala knew she had to shake it off and let it go. She had bigger things to worry about. One being the mysterious visit she had with Randstad; two, how the great detectives were getting along solving the murder cases; and three, finally getting her mother home. Nala knew how to deal with Kendrick and Crystal, and she decided it had to be done. She had no problem getting rid of and disposing of trash. It was something she had become quite fond of.

# Chapter 2

When Nala awoke the next afternoon, there was an empty bottle and a half of wine on her bed. She sat up in bed, rubbing her head and moaning at the pounding headache she had. The TV was playing some porn as Nala pulled the dildo from under the covers. It had become her man since Kendrick left. Nala didn't mind getting horny from watching porn and pleasing herself. She actually thought the dildo was the perfect man. It gets her off, then she washes it and puts it away. There were no arguments, compromises or lies. She liked it that way.

Nala slowly turned her head to the clock on her nightstand. It read 1:10 p.m., and she knew she needed to get up and move around. Nala slowly swung her feet off the bed and stood up. Her head was spinning as she walked to the bathroom and turned on the shower. She pulled off her nightshirt and stepped in, allowing the cool water to hit her face. It felt good as she let it run down her body for a few minutes before washing herself. When she finished, she got out to dry off. She took the Tylenol out of the medicine cabinet and swallowed two with a glass of water.

Nala looked at herself in the mirror and thought about her visit from Kendrick yesterday. She couldn't believe how he continuously thought she cared about him or Crystal. His visit just made her angrier and more bitter. With Crystal being pregnant and Nala possibly running into her at work made her blood boil. The last thing she wanted to see was

9

that pregnant bitch walking around like she had the perfect life. Everything she had she stole.

Nala went back into her bedroom and turned off the TV. She sat on the side of the bed and picked up her cell phone. There were a few missed calls and some voice messages. Nala began listening to them. As expected, there was one from Detective Chase. He had phoned several days prior in hopes she would help with the latest murder. His message reminded her of the mementos she had in her bureau. Nala got up and walked over to the bureau and opened it. She pulled out a red metal box and went back to sit on her bed. Nala opened it and looked at the treasures she had inside. The latest treasure instantly gave her an adrenaline rush. The thought of what she had done fulfilled her more than her dildo did the night before. After looking through the box, she placed it back in the bureau. Nala decided to give the detective a call to appease him, but she would do that later. Right now, she had something else she needed to do.

***

Nala had been at the mall for about an hour before she picked out a baby doll. She went back to her car and pulled it out of the bag, looking it over. It was a pretty black doll baby with curly hair. When she thought about Crystal carrying Kendrick's child, she began to stab the doll with her butcher knife repeatedly. Afterward, she removed the eyes and cut off the hands and feet. Although she would never hurt a baby, she wasn't too keen on Crystal having a happy-go-lucky pregnancy. In her eyes, Crystal was just as guilty as Kendrick. It takes two to cheat, and Crystal knew he was married. She was the ultimate homewrecker. Befriend the wife, then sleep with her man. Nala thought to herself that Crystal was more than deserving of a little stalking and fear.

After Nala parked a few blocks away from Kendrick's place, she got out of the car and went to the trunk to get her wig and shades. It was dark, and there were no people moving about in the neighborhood. She slipped on her wig and combed it before putting on the shades and black leather gloves. Afterward, she picked up the beautifully wrapped box and got out of the car. As she walked toward the house, she looked around to make sure no one would see her. With her fast pace, she was at the house in no time. Nala walked up on the porch and sat the box in front of the door. She walked over to the bay window and looked inside. It was evident no one was home by the dark house. Nala quickly left the porch and went back to the car. She felt like this was the beginning of a long, painful pregnancy for Crystal, and that made her happy.

## Chapter 3

When Nala pulled into her driveway, she didn't know what she was feeling. However, she did know eventually Kendrick would contact her with suspicions that she was the culprit who left the baby doll. They had no evidence and couldn't prove it was her. For all he knew, his beloved Crystal was sleeping around with someone else's man and pissed them off.

Nala sat in her car for a while before getting out and going into her house. Oftentimes, she thought about selling it and downsizing to a smaller place. But, when she thought about her plans of having her mother come to live with her, she dismissed the thought. She was going to do all she needed to do to have her mother come home to her. She needed her because they were alike. She loved the woman whom she called mom for years, but there was something about Dominique that connected with her. Maybe it was because they were both murderers. Or maybe it was because they seemed to enjoy being a murderer.

Nala went into her kitchen, took a wine glass from the cupboard, and then walked to her office. She sat behind her desk and filled her glass with the red wine that sat on her desk. Nala drank it down like it was a glass of cold water on a hot day. It felt refreshing as she wiped the wine from her mouth. Nala poured another glass, then turned on her computer. She opened her email and had over three hundred unread ones. Nala wasn't up to checking any of them, so she drank her second glass of wine and poured herself a third glass. She leaned her head back on the chair and closed her eyes. Nala could feel herself dozing as her body began to relax. She knew sleep was approaching as her arm dropped from the armrest of the chair. She sat up and drank the remaining wine in her glass. She turned off her computer, grabbed the bottle of wine, and headed upstairs.

The hallway seemed extra-long as she walked to her bedroom. Nala stumbled in the dark while she reached for the light in her room. She flipped up the switch and walked over to her bed. For the first time in a long time, she felt lonely. The house felt like it had no heart, and that made it extra cold to her. She poured another glass of wine and drank most of it before sitting the glass on her nightstand. Nala laid down on the bed and stared at the ceiling. Her eyes blinked slowly, turning the room light then dark. Without much effort, she was asleep.

Nala was awakened by loud banging on her bedroom door. She quickly sat up, startled as she looked around the room. She had no gun, but she did have an iron baseball bat. Nala's heart beat frantically as the banging got louder. Fear invaded her body as she sat frozen on the bed. She looked at the clock on her nightstand, and it read 3:20 am. Nala slowly got out of the bed, picked up the bat beside her nightstand, and tiptoed to the door. She listened to see if she heard any type of movement. There was none. Nala stood there, scared to move. Slowly, she put her hand on the doorknob and turned it. She could feel the big knot in her throat growing as her hand began to tremble. Nala breathed heavily with the sound filling her quiet room.

Beginning to feel sweat building on her forehead, she opened the door to no one standing there. She poked her head carefully out the door and looked down the hall. Still feeling shaken, she quietly left the room. She was afraid to go into the other rooms, but she knew she needed to if she was going to feel safe. Nala carefully entered each room and searched them. Afterward, she walked slowly down the steps and looked around while holding onto the baseball bat tightly. She then went into each room and found nothing. She checked the alarm, and it was still on with no evidence of it having been tampered with. Nala was perplexed because of the loud banging on her door. She knew she wasn't dreaming because the sound awoke her.

Nala went back upstairs, still feeling on edge, and went into her bedroom. She locked the door and quickly got into bed under her covers. The time read 3:40, and for some reason, Nala had an eerie feeling overcome her. It felt as if someone was in the room watching her. Nala reached for the wine bottle on her nightstand and opened it. She sat up in bed and drank the remaining wine from the bottle. Then, she put the bottle back and laid down. She couldn't shake the feeling that made her completely uncomfortable. Nala glanced around the room, then closed her eyes, trying to fall asleep. The house had a deathly silence that made the hair on the back of her neck stand up. Although her house was usually silent during that time of the morning, this silence was different. It was as if time was at a standstill. Nala didn't know why she had this feeling, but she wanted it to be over. She closed her eyes again and longed for sleep.

When Nala got to work, she was tired. She hadn't slept like she wanted, and, for the remainder of the night, she felt like someone was in her bedroom watching her. Nala walked into her office and plopped down on the chair behind her desk. She put her head down and let out a big sigh. As her eyes slowly began to close, her secretary walked in with a cup of hot coffee, just the way she liked it.

"You're a Godsend," she said, sitting up and taking the cup.

"No problem, Dr. Jordan. Can I get you anything else?"

"No, thank you."

Nala turned on her computer and sipped her coffee. It felt good as the warm liquid slid down her throat. Nala began looking through her emails when suddenly she looked up and saw two gentlemen approaching her office. She knew they were detectives because she could smell their badges and attitudes a million miles away. Nala immediately began to wonder if somewhere along her murder spree she slipped up. She was always as careful as she could be. Her disguise was on point, and it revealed no similarities to her true identity.

"Remain calm," she told herself as they got closer.

Nala didn't want them to notice her watching them, so she lowered her eyes back to the computer screen. When they arrived at Sonia's desk, one of them spoke as she stood up. Nala secretly looked up and quickly lowered her eyes again when Sonia entered the office.

"Dr. Jordan, there are some detectives here to see you. They say it's in reference to Professor Jordan."

"Okay. Send them in."

Sonia gestured for the detectives to enter as Nala stood up. She fixed her form-fitting dress, which was hugging her curves. Two detectives walked in, but one really caught her eye. He looked to be about six feet tall with a dark complexion and bald head. He had a neatly trimmed goatee with a small beard. When he unfastened his jacket, the muscles in his chest were well defined through his black shirt. Nala tried to daydream about what he looked like naked. She felt herself drifting away with her thoughts before she snapped herself back.

"Hello, Dr. Jordan, I'm Detective Washington, and this is Detective Jackson. We are with the Media Police Department," said the one she was admiring.

"Media Police Department? Is this about a case?"

"No. It's about a complaint that was filed against you by Mr. Kendrick Jordan and Ms. Crystal Carter. May we sit, please?

"Sure."

They all sat down as Nala took a few sips of her coffee. She knew she couldn't show any signs of worry. It was time to pull out the dumb girl, cute card and act oblivious.

"Did something happen to Crystal or Kendrick? "

"Well, not exactly. Someone left a very disturbing package on the porch of Mr. Jenkins and Ms. Carter."

"Really? What?" she asked curiously.

Detective Jackson, who didn't seem impressed with Nala's looks or position, leaned forward and firmly placed a picture on her desk in front of her. Nala could sense his negative disposition as she picked up the picture and looked at it. She felt herself wanting to laugh because she knew she'd gotten to Crystal, but she couldn't.

"What is this?" she asked.

"It's a picture of a doll that has been decapitated and dismembered. Do you know anything about that, Dr. Jordan?" Detective Jackson asked.

"No. Why, should I"?

"I don't know, you tell us. According to Ms. Carter and Mr. Jenkins, you have been harassing them since they became engaged and Ms. Carter learned of her pregnancy," Detective Jackson said with conviction.

"Harassing? Whether you know it or not, I am a very busy woman. I have no time for childish games."

"Well, you may be busy, but anyone who has been left for the side piece, who is now pregnant, would find the time to harass."

"Excuse me, you're out of line talking to me that way," Nala said angrily, standing up with her hands on her hip.

Detective Washington looked at his partner with disappointment as he sat with a smirk on his face.

"Detective Jackson, I need for you to take a walk."

Detective Jackson stood up and looked Nala in the eyes. She had never met him before, but she could feel his hate for her spewing from his body. Where did it come from? She had no clue, but if his behavior continued the way it was going, she would take a break from killing married men just to kill him.

"I apologize for Detective Jackson's behavior. Please sit down. Please."

"He was way out of line, and I'm thinking about making a complaint against him. What he said to me was totally unacceptable."

"I agree, and I'm sorry."

"You know what. Let's cut to the chase since you guys came here privy to the information involving the triangle comprised of Mr. Jenkins, Ms. Carter and myself. Yes, I'm still married to Mr. Jenkins, but hopefully not for long. Ms. Carter was his secretary before they started boning one another. Everyone knew but me, but when I found out, I threw his ass out. She's pregnant, they're getting married, and I'm fine. Was I angry in the beginning? Of course. Hurt? Yes. But I'm good now."

"They seem to think you're behind this latest incident. Ms. Carter said you threatened her in the parking lot at work."

"She's delusional. Maybe she got me mixed up with another man's wife," she said sarcastically.

"I don't know. They were both pretty shaken up, especially her since she's pregnant."

"Detective Washington, I'm sure you may know I'm a very busy woman. I'm the head of this department, I do speaking engagements, I help law enforcement across the country profile killers, and I'm currently helping the Philadelphia Police Department solve the murders sweeping their city by a serial killer. I'm sure you heard of their problem over there. As you can see, I have no time for other 'recreation.' I had nothing to do with this butchered doll, and I'm sorry you had to waste your time coming here."

"Oh, I know your work and what you do. It wasn't a waste. We received a complaint, and we followed up. So, when was the last time you saw either Mr. Jenkins or Ms. Carter?"

"Uh, I really can't remember. I may occasionally bump into them on campus, but that's rare, being we work on different sides of the campus."

"I see. Did you ever go to their home and threaten them?"

"No."

"Ms. Carter says you stalked her...."

"Stalked?" Nala asked, laughing. "Does she really think she's that important to me?"

"Okay, for a better choice of words, she says you approached her in the parking lot one night and threatened her and her mother. Any truth to that?"

Nala sat and looked at Detective Washington for a second. She was quickly taken back to the conversation she had with her mother in California. Her mother told her to let Crystal and Kendrick know she was there. She also told her to make their lives a living hell. Mission accomplished. It made her feel good to know they were both scared. She wanted them to feel what she felt upon returning home and finding them in her bed. She wanted them to feel what it was like to be humiliated. Nala was finally getting them back, and she wasn't done, not by a long shot.

"No, detective, there's no truth to that. Now, are we done? I have to really get back to work."

"Yes, we're done," he said, standing up. "Thank you for your time, and I apologize once again for Detective Jackson's behavior."

"No need to apologize for him. You were the perfect gentleman."

"Thank you."

The two looked at each other for a second before it became awkward, and they turned away. Nala had noticed the wedding band on his finger when he first entered the office, so he was off-limits unless he crossed the line. However, she did find him extremely attractive, and he seemed kind, unlike his shitty-ass partner. Detective Washington put his notepad in his pocket and extended his hand to her for a handshake. His hands were moist, and his nails were neatly manicured. She was turned on by the pride he evidently took in his appearance.

"If there's anything else, I will contact you," he said.

"There shouldn't be, but if by chance Ms. Carter has another complaint, please be sure to visit me without your partner."

"Duly noted. Once again, thank you."

Detective Washington walked out of the office as Nala stood watching him. She saw Detective Jackson appear, and the two walked away together. Nala sat down and immediately contacted her connect, so she could speak to her mother later. She had to tell her what was going on.

Detective Washington could sense his partner's disapproval as they walked to the car. When they got in, Detective Jackson turned and looked at him. They had been partners for the last five years, and it was always the good cop, bad cop routine with Detective Washington. At times, it worked, but other times it was annoying.

"What was that back there?" Detective Jackson angrily asked.

"Police work."

"Police work? Really? Man, she was ready to file a complaint against you. Don't you have enough of them already?"

"Listen, I know she's pretty as hell with a bad body, so your thinking isn't clear. But there's something about her, and I sensed it right off the bat."

"You sensed what? We hadn't even been in there five minutes before you went in on her. So, what did you sense?"

"It doesn't take a rocket scientist to know she's bitter. Her husband cheated on her, left her for the side chick, got her pregnant, and now he's going to marry her. Shit, I'd be pissed too and ready to make somebody pay."

"That doesn't mean she did anything. Next time, get some facts before you make a judgment call."

"Okay, cool. But are you feeling her, Jackson?"

"Man, what? Naw, I'm not feeling her. I don't even know her. This is business, okay?"

"Well, all jokes aside, if you were feeling her, it would be okay. Diane wouldn't mind. She would think it was time, and she would be happy."

"Man, what are you talking about? It's work, that's all."

"Do you think she's pretty?"

Detective Jackson chuckled like a schoolboy. He did find Nala attractive, but his heart was still with his wife, Diane. She was the love of his life, and he didn't want to dishonor that. He still loved her very much.

"We're not doing this. Stick to the facts, okay?"

"Yeah, okay. And what are the facts?"

"She said she didn't do any of the things she's accused of."

"Ha! That's what all guilty people say."

Detective Jackson shook his head at Detective Washington and pulled off. Secretly, Detective Jackson was hoping it wasn't over. He did want to see Nala again. It made him feel disloyal to Diane for being attracted to another woman, but it had been two years since she died. Within that time, he never looked at another woman, had sex or even dated. He didn't know how to feel about what he was feeling. After all, he had just laid eyes on Nala for the first time today. He was hoping it was just a quick physical attraction that would go away. If it wasn't, he didn't know what he was going to do.

# Chapter 4

The day had gone fairly smooth for Nala. She was feeling like a winner knowing Kendrick and Crystal were scared. Being scared meant they were thinking about her. Being scared meant they had no clue of her stability. Most importantly for Nala, being scared meant she was in control. She was in control of their thoughts, their actions, the way they planned their day and how safe they felt throughout the day. It was a victory for her. Nala didn't want either of them to have any peace. Knowing Crystal was pregnant had no bearing on her. In her opinion, there were casualties of war, and this was war. If a miscarriage was to happen, so be it. When Nala found out about the pregnancy, she didn't want any harm to come to the baby. She felt that way up until a few days ago when she purchased the baby doll. Nala wasn't concerned about the outcome of harassing them would have on Crystal. Her primary motive was to evoke fear in them, and so far, she had accomplished that.

Nala pulled around to the front of her house and parked. She began thinking about Detective Jackson and how handsome he was. Nala hadn't been with a man sexually in a long time, but thinking about him made her horny. She could visualize herself sitting on his hard, erect dick while his strong arms held her waist and guided her strokes. Nala hoped to see him again, but she knew she couldn't see him in the way she was thinking. After all, he was a married man, and she didn't want to have to kill him for being unfaithful. However, there was nothing wrong with fantasizing. She shook off the thought and grabbed her briefcase before getting out of the car. It had gotten colder since the sun set.

All Nala wanted to do was get inside, get out of her clothes, and put on her warm pajamas. Nala walked to her door and unlocked it. Once inside, she set the alarm and threw her keys on the table in the hall. She unzipped her boots and took them off, leaving them beside the table as well. Nala headed to the kitchen and filled her teapot with water. She sat it on the stove and turned it on before getting a mug from the cabinet. Nala sat at the kitchen table and began fidgeting through her phone. As the water was beginning to boil on the stove, Nala got up to get an herbal tea bag from the container where she kept her various flavored teas. She put the teabag in the mug and walked back over to the stove. She could hear the water boiling inside as the whistle made its way to the tip of the sprout. Nala let it whistle for a second before turning off the stove and pouring some water into the mug.

Afterward, she went to sit back at the table. Nala put one teaspoon of sugar and honey in her tea. She sipped it slowly as the hotness touched the brim of her upper lip. Nala thought to herself how good the warm tea tasted. She got up and went into her office. Nala sat her mug down on the desk and walked over to her fireplace. It wasn't a real fireplace, but the logs gave off heat like it was. She sat down behind her desk and turned on her computer, going directly to her email. She scrolled through until she saw a message from her contact. She opened the message which read, "call me." Nala quickly dialed her number from the cell phone she used to speak to her mother, Dominique. Her contact answered on the second ring.

"Hey, what's up? Is everything alright?" Nala curiously asked.

"Actually, everything is great. I have some good news for you."

"What!?" Nala anxiously asked.

"Your mother is going to be released. They had her hearing this past week, and she has been granted parole. I didn't want to say anything until it was official, and it was a done deal."

Nala felt her body become overheated as she tried to digest what she had just been told. After over thirty-five years, her mother was going to be coming home. Nala was happy, but she was feeling some other stuff too. She couldn't explain it, but it felt weird and good. Nala was speechless as she heard the woman calling her name.

"Yes, I'm here. This is all so overwhelming. So, when does she come home?"

"Well, paperwork can be crazy and tedious, so probably within a few weeks. I'm glad you called because I was going to actually call you. They're going to need a person to who your mother will be released. Will that be you?"

"Absolutely, yes! Anything you need, just tell me."

"More than likely, they will want to meet or talk with you. Forward me your information, and I will make sure the powers that be get it."

"I want to go and get her, so I can meet with them face to face. Just let me know when."

"Oh, ok. I didn't think that was an option, but since it is, I will let them know. As soon as I hear when they want to meet and her actual release date, I will contact you. And Nala, no need to call me on this secure line anymore. Your mother is technically a free woman. Also, one of the reasons your mother is getting released is because she helped bust an ongoing prostitution ring within the facility. Dr. Jacobs was charged with solicitation of prostitution, along with other numerous charges."

"What!!!! Did my mother...."

"No. But she played the part. She's a brave woman. We'll be able to talk more in detail later. Why don't you marinate on your mother coming home first."

"Okay, but is she safe?"

"Yes, she is. I promise you. You can talk to her tomorrow."

Nala talked to her contact for another fifteen minutes before hanging up. She was so excited, she was beside herself. Nala was anxious about having her mother come home. She had so many emotions going on she felt overwhelmed. Nala got up and went into the den and got a bottle of red wine. She popped it open with the cork and poured herself a glass. Nala drank half of it and went back into her office. She sat the bottle down on her desk and stared at the screen of her computer. A smile came over her face again as she finished the wine in her glass. She poured some more and sat back in her chair, resting her head back. Although Nala loved and appreciated the woman she called mom all her life, she had a mental connection with her mother. It was as if they knew what one another was thinking and feeling. Nala felt that was because she and her mother were cut from the same cloth. There was a bond they shared, which was more than mother and daughter. In the little time she had known her, she felt more in tune with her than she ever did her other mother.

Nala sipped more of her wine and sat up going through the rest of her messages. She saw a few from Detective Chase she knew she should read. Although she had taken a hiatus from killing, they hadn't taken one from trying to find her. Nala was starting to feel the effects of the wine. She shut her computer down, picked up the bottle and her glass, and left her office. Before going upstairs, she checked the alarm system to ensure the house was secure. When she got to her bedroom, she turned on the TV and plopped down on the bed. There was nothing of interest to her as she flipped through what seemed like a million channels. Nala turned on the ID channel and began watching "Deadly Women." That was one of her favorite shows to watch. Before she began killing, she couldn't believe how evil and calculating the women she saw on the show were. However, after her first kill, she realized all killers aren't evil. Sometimes, in her opinion, they were drawn to do it. It was either by circumstances or their DNA. Nala was intrigued by the episode she was watching. It was great entertainment for her. As her interest grew deeper in the show, her cell phone began to buzz.

Chuckling, she looked at the phone and contemplated answering it, but she didn't really want to interrupt her flow. She was feeling good. Nala sent the call to voicemail and continued watching her show. For the next ten minutes, her cell phone continued to vibrate with an incoming call. By this time, Nala had almost finished her wine, and she was up for the challenge. She answered the phone with a relaxed tone.

"Yes," she said.

"I'm not supposed to call you, but I needed to. Crystal and I know it was you that left the doll on our porch. Why are you so fuckin mean?"

"Kendrick, I don't know what you're talking about. What doll?" she asked, playing coy.

"Okay, I get it, Nala! I get it! I hurt you, I did you wrong, and I have said sorry over and over again. I tried to make things right again between us, but you kept pushing me away. After getting told countless times to leave you alone, I did. Now I'm with Crystal, and you want to try and hurt our baby. What did the baby do to you!"

"Kendrick, obviously you are delusional. I don't know why you and your, uh, girl, think I have time to devote to bothering y'all. You keep barking up the wrong tree and soon it's going to bite back."

"Are you threatening me?"

Nala laughed out loud and looked at the phone. She knew what Kendrick was trying to do. After all, everyone knew who had the true brains in the relationship. Nala wasn't going to fall for his bait of getting her to confess to anything. She was fully aware he was probably taping her, thinking she would incriminate herself. He should have known she was far from stupid. But Nala figured she would play his game for a little longer because it amused her.

"Of course, I'm not threatening you, Kendrick. Why would I want to do that? You got me pegged all wrong."

"Oh, do I? I don't think so. Listen, I didn't set out to hurt you; I really didn't. I loved you. You know that. Sometimes, I sit back and think about things, and I know I fucked up. All I can say is I'm sorry, again. But I need you to chill with trying to hurt Crystal. There's more at stake now."

"Of course, it is; she's pregnant. You have to take care of her to make sure she stays healthy and strong, so she can have a big, bouncing baby when it's time. I'm sure you'll do that. Won't you, Kendrick?"

"That's what I'm trying to do, okay, Nala. I'm just saying, if you're trying to get back at me by getting back at Crystal, please stop."

"I hear you. Now, I have to go. You're interrupting my TV flow. I'm watching Deadly Women. This one is about this woman who killed her ex-husband and his girlfriend. And get this, the chick was pregnant. Have a good night, Kendrick."

Nala pushed the button to end the call and tossed the phone back on the bed. She laughed out as she watched TV and drank her wine.

Kendrick felt sick to his stomach as he sat in his car looking at his phone. He felt a coldness from Nala that sent shivers through his body. She had been giving him that feeling lately with her words and lack of emotion. He didn't know how he could get through to her. Kendrick thought about going to speak to her parents, but he was sure he wasn't one of their favorite people. Calling Nala's friend Pam was out of the question, as well. She hated him just as much. He felt stuck, but he knew he needed to do something.

Crystal had really been rattled by the doll incident. She had stayed in bed the next day because she felt sick and started to spot blood. When Kendrick took her to the emergency room, the doctor said she was stressed and needed to rest, but there was no immediate danger to the baby. That hit too close to home for Kendrick, and that was why they filed the police report. However, he felt like Nala wasn't going to give up, but he couldn't prove she was doing anything wrong. It was his word against hers until he could catch her. Catching her, however, wasn't going to be easy. Kendrick knew Nala was the best criminal psychologist on this side of town. She knew how to read people, what they were thinking, and what made them tick. Hell, he knew she was cautious in her responses to him. But he just hoped sooner or later she would slip up; the best of them always do.

When Kendrick got in the house, Crystal was lying on the couch in the living room, snuggled under a big quilt. She looked scared and worried. He looked at her, and, at that time, he realized he didn't love her. Sometimes, he didn't like her, but he tolerated her. In his mind, she was the reason he was no longer with Nala, his soulmate. Although he had fucked up several times before by stepping out of his marriage, he always knew Nala was the only woman he ever would truly love. She was the only woman who would wear his last name. Kendrick knew it was probably too late for him and Nala, and that was something he had to live with. For now, Crystal was a convenience. She was someone he could fuck whenever he wanted, someone who would tend to his every need, and occasionally he could take out in public as his trophy. She could look pretty but not talk too much. He did care for her, and now even more than before, because she was carrying his child. He knew he would never marry her, but as long as she thought so, she would stick around. Kendrick walked over to her and sat down. She moved next to him and put her head on his shoulder. He knew how much she loved him, and he needed her to think he felt the same way, at least until the baby was born.

"How you feel"? he asked her.

"Better now that you're home. I really couldn't sleep. Kept thinking I heard someone outside," she nervously said.

"No one is outside. Everything is cool. You're gonna have to try and relax. Stop stressing."

Crystal sat up and looked at Kendrick with a shocked look on her face. She couldn't believe he said that. It almost sounded as if he was blaming her for being scared when Nala was the culprit. When Crystal looked at him, he had a disgusted look on his face, like he was tired of her. She hoped for their sake he was tired of the situation Nala was putting them in, but she couldn't tell. At times, Crystal felt Kendrick loved her, but at other times she was unsure. This moment proved her uncertainty.

"Stop stressing? How do I do that when I have a crazy-ass woman stalking me?"

"Come on, Crystal, crazy? Nala isn't crazy. Mad maybe, but not crazy."

"Well, what do you call someone who gift wraps a baby doll, dismembers it and then sends it to a pregnant woman? That sounds like crazy to me."

"Listen, all I'm saying is you have to chill. Every little bump or noise isn't someone out to get you. Relax. It's not good for the baby."

Crystal stood up and tossed the blanket off her. She was starting to get angry as she listened to Kendrick. She couldn't figure out where it was coming from. Had he talked to Nala? Did she persuade him it wasn't her? And most importantly, did he believe her? Kendrick had a nonchalant look on his face that hurt Crystal. What was his reasoning behind being so cold and insensitive? Crystal hated to think that he still loved Nala.

"I know it's not good for the baby. I also know everyone isn't out to get me. That's reserved for just one person, Nala!"

"Damn Crystal, stop acting like the victim. What happened to that feisty, cutthroat, I don't care chick that went after a married man and got him? You can deal with this."

Crystal's eyes welled up, and, as much as she didn't want to cry, she couldn't control it. The tears began to fall heavily down her face. The tears were so strong they impaired her vision, and Kendrick looked like a painting that had gotten wet with the paint beginning to run. Crystal turned, holding her stomach, and quickly headed upstairs. Kendrick could hear her crying as she walked down the hall and slammed the door to their bedroom. He took his cellphone out of his pocket and pulled up Nala's phone number. He clicked on the picture next to her name and enlarged it. She looked so sexy to him that he got an instant hard-on. He didn't know how much longer he could hide how he truly felt. He wanted his wife back, but he also wanted to have his child with Crystal. Kendrick knew he was fucked.

***

Nala had fallen asleep after watching a marathon of Deadly Women. She laughed as she drifted off, calling them "her sisters." Sleep had come rather quickly after she closed her eyes. She was deep into sleep when she was awakened by a loud bang on her door. Nala jumped up and was startled as she looked around the room. Her eyes were blurry as she rubbed them, trying to bring them into focus. Nala looked at the clock on the nightstand that read 3:20 am. The banging became louder in her ears. Nala's heart began to pound faster as she reached for the metal bat on her nightstand. She slowly stood up and quietly walked to her bedroom door. Her palms began to sweat, and she could hear the rhythm of her heartbeat as she approached the door.

"Bang, Bang, Bang," the sound roared while Nala stood once again, frozen in fear. She was sure she had secured the house, so who had gotten in? Nala didn't know what to do. She slowly put her ear to the door, trying to determine if she could hear movement. Nothing.

The banging began again, and this time Nala screamed. She ran back to her nightstand and got her phone. She immediately dialed 911.

"911, what's your emergency?"

"Please, someone is in my house outside of my bedroom door. Please send someone," Nala whispered.

"Okay, ma'am. How many are there?"

"I don't know. I'm in my bedroom. They started banging on my door. Please, hurry!"

"Okay, ma'am, calm down. Stay where you are, and I'm sending a car to you now. Are you able to see the siren lights from where you are?"

"Yes. I'll be able to."

"Okay. Do not come out of your bedroom until you see the siren lights."

"Please hurry! Please!" she said frantically.

"Ma'am, someone is on the way now. I'll stay on the line with you and wait until the car arrives to let you know it's safe."

"Thank you, thank you!"

Nala huddled between her bed and the nightstand holding the bat tightly. The banging had finally stopped, but she was still scared. The dispatcher on the phone reassured her everything would be okay. Her voice soothed her, and Nala began to feel relaxed. After what seemed like an eternity, the dispatcher finally told Nala the police were at her front door. Nala could see the lights blaring like she was at a concert. She got up slowly and walked to the bedroom door.

Nala held the bat as she turned the knob. She stuck her head out of her room, then quickly ran down the hallway and down the stairs. Nala opened the door, and two officers entered the house. She let out a sigh of relief as she ran into the arms of one of the male officers. He assured her she was safe as they walked further in. He informed her there were two officers outside checking the perimeter of the house.

"Ma'am, you're safe. Officer Wincoat is going to talk to you while I check the home. From what we can see, there's no one here."

"Can we sit, please?" asked the officer while her partner began his search of the house. "What happened?" she asked as they walked into the living room to sit down.

"I, uh, I was awakened again by someone banging on my door."

"Again? This happened before?" asked the officer.

"Yes, last night. There was a loud banging on my bedroom door. I got up, grabbed my bat and slowly left my room to search the house."

"Did you see anything out of the ordinary?"

"No. Nothing was touched, and my alarm system was still on."

"So, tell me again, what happened?"

"I was asleep, and all of a sudden there was a loud bang. I jumped up and looked at the clock and it was 3:20. I left my room and searched the house."

"So, what made you call the police tonight and not last night?"

"I don't know. Last night was the first time it happened, so I just let it go. But then, it happened again tonight. I wanted to be sure there was no one here."

"Okay, no problem. I'll be right back."

The officer walked away. Nala could tell she thought she was looney. Whatever the case, she wanted to be sure there was no one somehow getting into her house and scaring her. She walked over to the glass bureau and took out a bottle of wine and a glass. She poured it half full and took a big swallow. The officer looked over at her out of the corner of her eye and continued talking. Nala didn't care what she thought of her, just as long as they found no evidence of anyone being at her house.  Nala finished the wine in the glass and poured another. She went back to sit down and waited for the officer to come back. Nala was afraid of guns, but she was considering getting one more and more. She had no clue what was happening, but something was happening. The two officers walked over to her as she drank her wine in one swallow.

"Ma'am, we checked the entire house and grounds and found no evidence of anyone trying to enter your home."

"Okay, well, I needed to know for sure."

"You told Officer Wincoat that this happened last night. Is it possible you're dreaming, and it just seems very real?"

"No, I'm not dreaming. I'm fully awake when the banging occurs. It wakes me up, and it continues while I'm awake. It's not a dream."

"Fine, no problem. Well, as I stated, we checked your house thoroughly and there was nothing. Just make sure you turn on your alarm system, and, if anything else happens, don't hesitate to give us a call."

"Thank you," Nala said, getting up and leading them to the front door. Although they found nothing, she felt safe that they had come out. The officers said their goodbyes, and Nala closed the door and turned on the alarm system. She turned off the lights, except the light in the hallway. Afterward, she went upstairs to her bedroom and closed the door, locking it.

Nala climbed into bed and turned on the TV. She hoped it would put her to sleep. Whatever was going on, she needed someone else to witness it with her. She told herself later that morning she would call Pam and invite her for a sleepover. If the banging happened again, someone else would hear it, and she wouldn't think that maybe she was going crazy.

## Chapter 5

Crystal was up early that morning in the kitchen. She had made herself a cup of herbal tea with lemon. Crystal needed time to think about Kendrick's attitude and response to her about being scared. The night for her wasn't pleasant as she tossed and turned, trying to sleep. She noticed Kendrick hadn't come to bed until the early morning hours. She didn't want to fight with Kendrick or be angry. She truly loved him and was happy she was carrying his baby. However, she knew how she got him was foul. Was the stalking and Kendrick's cold attitude a result of that? She knew how real karma was. She had experienced her firsthand before moving to Pennsylvania. That was something from her past she hoped would never follow her.

Crystal sipped on her tea and tried to put herself in a better mood. She hoped that would be enough for Kendrick to shatter his icy attitude towards her and become loving again. She had finished her tea by the time Kendrick came downstairs dressed for work. There was a cup of hot coffee waiting for him on the kitchen table.

Kendrick walked into the kitchen, then strode over to Crystal and took her by the hand. He gently pulled her from the chair and hugged her. Crystal returned the hug tightly as she buried her face in his chest. He kissed her on the top of her head and sat down at the kitchen table.

"I'm sorry about yesterday. I know you're scared. I just don't want you to worry yourself and bring stress to the baby. We contacted the police, and I'm sure they spoke to her already. You'll probably hear from them today. Just relax."

"I'll try, Kendrick."

"Okay. So, I'm about to go. Getting back to work will be good for you too."

"Yeah, I know. I'm due back Monday."

"Cool."

Kendrick sipped a little more of his coffee and got up to leave the kitchen. Crystal followed behind him with a big smile. She felt better and hoped his apology was sincere. Kendrick put on his coat, and Crystal handed him his briefcase. He kissed her on the lips and left out of the house. Crystal closed the door behind him and went back into the kitchen.

After getting in his car, Kendrick took out his cellphone. He pulled up the picture of Nala again and looked at it. Getting her back was his focus, and making Crystal think they were good until the baby was born was how he would do it.

Nala had gotten to work early that morning and took a nap on the sofa in her office. It was the first time she had slept comfortably in the last two days. She hoped when she called Pam to ask if she would stay the weekend, she would. Nala sat up, stretching and feeling more rested, and went into her bathroom inside her office. She brushed her teeth and got dressed for the day. When she finished, she sat behind her desk and turned on the computer. She could see her secretary coming in, carrying a cup holder. Nala knew it was her caramel-flavored coffee with whipped cream and caramel drippings. She smiled when Sonia entered her office and handed her the good-smelling, hot cup.

"Thank you sooooo much. You don't know how much I need this."

"No problem. How are you today?"

"I'm okay. Just haven't had much sleep in the last few nights. Other than that, I'm good."

"That's good. Well, if you need anything, just buzz."

"Okay, and thanks again."

"You're welcome," Sonia said, leaving the office.

Nala closed her eyes and sipped the coffee. The aroma mesmerized her as she took another sip and smiled. She was feeling better, but she was excited about calling her mother today. Having her home would be such a good thing for them. She hadn't told the mother who raised her yet what was going on. When she thought about it, she realized she hadn't even spoken to her in a while. She knew she needed to call her. Without her and her dad raising her and taking care of her, there's no telling where she would be. She owed them her life and a debt of gratitude. She figured she would have them over for dinner next week to tell them what was going on. They needed to know her mother would be home soon. Nala knew that would bring major changes and adaptations for everyone. Her parents, at least, deserved the opportunity to digest and marinate on the situation.

She sat drinking her coffee and feeling like it was the best thing she ever tasted. Nala still had some time before her class started, so she dialed Pam's number. She answered, sounding a little concerned. She hadn't spoken to Nala in a few weeks, so she wasn't sure if everything was fine.

"Hey, Nala. Is everything okay?"

"Well, yeah and no. But first off, how are you?"

"I'm good. Just working. But cut the small talk, what's up?"

"Well, I was wondering if you wanted to stay with me for the weekend? We could watch movies, eat ice cream, and do girl stuff."

"Is something wrong?"

"Yeah, kind of. In a nutshell, there's been some strange things happening at my house. It got me so rattled I called the cops last night."

"Really? What happened?"

"I can't really go into detail because I have a class in about fifteen minutes. Just trust me when I say strange, and I'm a little spooked. I can tell you everything if you can come."

"Okay, it shouldn't be a problem. Just so happens Mike is going away with his frat brothers this weekend, so I was going to be alone anyway. I'll come over later tonight."

"Thanks, Pam, I appreciate it. And don't worry, you'll be safe. So, I'll see you later tonight?"

"Yeah. I'll call you in a few to let you know the definite time. But for now, I have to get out of here and get to work. Talk to you later."

"Okay. Love you, sis."

"Love you too."

Nala felt much better about having some company in the house with her for the weekend. Whatever was happening, she hoped Pam would be a witness to it as well.

After finishing her coffee, Nala gathered her belongings and headed to her class. When she arrived, Jessica was on her laptop scrolling. Nala sat her briefcase down on the podium and began to unpack it. Whatever had

Jessica's interest didn't allow her to look up. Nala cleared her throat and Jessica quickly looked up, startled.

"In deep thought, are we?"

"Oh, sorry Dr. Jordan. I didn't see you come in," she said apologetically.

"No problem."

Jessica sat desperately, wanting to ask Nala a question, but she wasn't sure how. She wanted to help Nala with the serial murders in Philly because she believed it could help her career. However, on a more personal note, she wanted to catch the killer because of her aunt being a victim of Robert Randstad. She cleared her throat and sat up straight like she was being scolded by the principal in his office.

"Uh, Dr. Jordan. Have you thought more about me helping with the serial murder case in Philadelphia?"

"Have I thought about it?" she asked, confused. "Was I supposed to?"

"Well, I just remember Detective Chase said it might be a good idea if I helped out. You know, maybe set some fresh eyes on the case."

Nala chuckled and walked toward Jessica, who was beginning to look a bit nervous. Although Nala hadn't killed in a while, she wasn't ready to have some eager young student trekking around her crime scene. When the idea was previously presented to her, she thought about using Jessica, but, in further thought, she believed it would be too risky.

"Jessica, I appreciate your willingness to want to help, but I don't think it's necessary. Your focus should be on finishing up this seminar class and moving on with your studies. I've got this under control."

41

"Please, Dr. Jordan. I don't have to get too involved with the case. I can do whatever you don't want to do. Make calls, research information, run errands, whatever. It would just be so good for me and where I'm trying to go in my career."

"And where is that?"

"I want to be like you."

"Hmmm, be careful what you wish for," Nala said with a smirk.

Jessica put her head down in disappointment, but she was curious what Nala meant by her statement. Although she said no for the time being, Jessica planned to revisit the conversation in hopes Nala would change her mind. Nala leaned against the podium as her students entered. This was a special research class in which there were only fifteen students enrolled. It was for three months, but it was worth five credits. The students in the class had been hand-selected by Nala. She believed they were the next group of brilliant-minded criminal psychologists. Nala understood why Detective Chase suggested Jessica help with the case. She had proven she was dedicated to the field, and also, she was on the road to becoming a great profiler.

The students sat and waited eagerly for what Nala had to say. Although they were in another class she taught, they felt extremely special and honored to be in this class.

"So, welcome. If you're sitting here listening to my voice, then I must think you're at the top of your game. I must see something that propels you above the rest of your classmates. Now that's not to say your other classmates are not academically inclined because they are, but you guys have something extra special. In this field, as you know, you have to have something special. A knack, if you will, for finding out how people tick. So, in this class, you will each be assigned a case where you will do a complete profile. Now, these cases are actual cases sent to me by law officials. If your profile leads to a suspect's capture and arrest, you know what that means. Publicity, opportunity, exposure for you and this department. So, without further ado, I will give you your assignments."

Nala stepped behind her podium and picked up the fifteen manila folders. They each had the name of a student on them. One by one, Nala called the students to the front of the class to receive their folders. She watched as they opened their folders and removed the information. The packet contained police reports, interviews, crime scene photos and other pertinent information. Nala specifically watched for Jessica's response. After removing the first sheet of information, Jessica excitedly looked up at Nala with a big smile. She had been given the case in which Nala was the perpetrator. Jessica couldn't understand why Nala hadn't just told her she would be profiling the case. Whatever the reason, she was ecstatic. Nala wanted to see just how good Jessica was. If, in fact, she did solve the case, Nala didn't think she would expose her. She had a connection from Jessica that had no feelings of betrayal attached to it. She felt safe having her investigate the murders that she committed. After class, Jessica walked up to Nala feeling very grateful.

"Thank you, Dr. Jordan. I had no idea," she said.

"How would you? So, let's see what you're made of."

"Do I get to work with you?"

"No. This is strictly solo. If you have questions, I may be able to answer them, but otherwise, this is you showing me what you can do."

"Okay. Well, thanks again. I'll make you proud."

"You're welcome, and let's see.

Nala headed back to her office to do a few things before heading out. She wanted to stop off at the store to pick up more wine and some groceries for her weekend with Pam. She was surprised to see Detective Jackson sitting in the lobby of the Psychology Department. Nala wondered if Kendrick and Crystal had sent him to her once again. Nala thought maybe she should take them both out, so they could leave her alone. As Nala approached him, she looked him over. He was definitely a handsome man. He looked to be about six-two and dark chocolate. He had a mustache with a very close-cut beard that was neatly groomed. What really made him look distinguished to her was the cleft in his chin. He was very well dressed in a charcoal gray suit with a lavender shirt and tie. In Nala's opinion, he looked like a runway model instead of a cop.

"Detective Jackson, to what do I owe the pleasure?" she said, extending her hand.

"Well, I just have a few more questions for you, if that's ok."

"I don't know what else I can tell you. Please, come in."

Nala walked into her office with the detective following behind her. She sat her belongings on her desk and gestured for him to have a seat. Nala sat down behind her desk and waited to hear what he had to say.

"So, I spoke to Mr. Jordan and Ms. Carter, and they still seem to think in some way you were behind the doll incident. Mr. Jordan accepted that we spoke to you, but Ms. Carter was more difficult to reassure."

"That is possibly due to her demons catching up to her. She needs to blame someone else for her shortcomings. As I told you and your partner, I had nothing to do with it."

"Okay, fine. Well, as it stands, we are still trying to find out who sent the package. It's about tracing steps, finding out where the dolls are sold, doing a little police work," he said, smiling.

"Well, I wish you luck. It's a shame you have to be bogged down with such a minor crime when your time could be spent on more important things."

"Well, Dr. Jordan, every crime is important to us, no matter how small."

"Hmmm." She looked at him. "So, if that's it, I have to do some work of my own," she said, standing up.

"Oh yes, that's it." He stood up. For a second, they both looked at each other with admiration but quickly dropped their eyes, followed by a nervous giggle. "I'll be in touch if need be."

"Sure, no problem. And by the way, thank you for not bringing your partner. I would have hated to take off my woman armor and become indignant."

"No problem. Thanks." He shook her hand and walked out. There was definitely an attraction, and Nala wondered how long it would be before someone made a move. She knew he was married and off-limits, but if the opportunity presented itself, she might have to bite.

***

Nala had been thinking about her visit from Detective Jackson. When she thought about it, it made no sense for him to come and see her. When he entered her office, he knew nothing, and when he left, he knew nothing. Nala wanted to believe it had something to do with him being attracted to her. If that was the case, it did make her smile.

When she entered the house, she set her bag down and went into the den. She wanted to call her mother, Dominique, before Pam arrived. Nala pulled out her phone and dialed the number. She sat on the sofa in the den and kicked off her pumps. Nala's face lit up like a Christmas tree when she heard her mother's voice on the other end.

"Hi, Mom," she said with excitement.

"Hi, honey. I'm so glad you called. I thought you forgot."

"Oh no, I didn't forget. It's just been a little crazy over here, that's all."

"What's wrong?"

"Nothing, nothing." She tried to sound convincing. "So, you're getting out? You're finally coming home?"

"Don't try and change the subject. I can feel something is wrong, or at least has you unsettled. What is it?"

"I just haven't been sleeping too well. Strange things have been happening, but everything is alright now."

"What kind of strange things?" her mother asked with concern.

"Well, for the last two nights, I've been awakened by a loud banging on my door. The first night, I was scared, but I searched the whole house, and it was fine. Last night, it happened again, but this time I was really spooked, so I called the cops. They came out, checked the house inside and out, and there was nothing.”

“Which door? Your front door?’

“No, my bedroom door.”

“Your bedroom door? Are you sure you weren’t dreaming?”

“I’m positive. It happened both nights at the same time.”

“What time?”

“3:20 a.m.”

There was a silence between the two as Nala could hear her mother breathing on the other end of the phone. She didn’t want to worry her by telling her, but Nala also knew her mother wouldn’t let up until she knew what was going on.

“Pay attention to that time. It means something, and soon it will be revealed. There is a story in that time, honey.”

“Come on, Mom. You sound all psychic. It’s fine.”

“Do as I say,” she said, raising her voice. “I’m sorry, honey. I didn’t mean to yell. Just listen to me. Pay attention to the time, okay.”

“Okay, Mom, I will.”

“Promise me,” she said as her voice cracked.

“I promise.”

Nala could feel her mother was very concerned for her. She did feel a spiritual connection to her when she visited her at the hospital. It was as if her mother knew things about her she shouldn’t have. To appease her, Nala would pay close attention to the time.

“So, how about that? I’m getting out of here.”

"Yes, I'm so glad. I'm waiting to hear when I can come pick you up. Hopefully, I'll hear something soon."

"What do you mean, pick me up?"

"Huh? Pick you up. Bring you home."

"Oh Nala, I'm not coming there. I don't think it's a good idea."

"What!? You're not coming here? What are you talking about? That's all we talked about when I was there visiting was having you home. Now, we have the chance, and you're saying you don't want to come here. Why?"

"Well, I thought about it, and your mother, my sister, and her husband did a wonderful job raising you. I owe them my life. You turned out to be such a beautiful woman in many ways. That's because of them. I don't want to step on anyone's toes by being there. I think it's best if I move somewhere else and start over. It'll be good for me."

"Wait a minute. What? You can't do that. I'm just starting to get to know you. I'm starting to see where I get certain attributes and qualities from. Yes, Mom and Dad have been the best. I owe them my life too, but you're my *Mom*. You were taken from me because of circumstances beyond your control. Please, don't make me lose you all over again."

"How do you think your mom will feel about that? After all, I haven't seen Josephine in years."

"She will be as happy as I am. She misses you too. She knows you shouldn't have been there, and I'm sure she will be ecstatic to see you. Just let me handle Mom and Dad. We're family, and family takes care of one another. I'm not going to have you gone for thirty years, get out and then go away for another thirty. Nope. So, when I get the green light, I'm coming to get you. Okay?"

"Well, what can I say? Okay."

"Great! Besides, it'll be good having someone here with me. Sometimes, this house feels so gigantic with just me here. I feel like I'm getting swallowed up sometimes. Now, it'll feel like a home again."

Nala's mother was happy she wanted her to stay because she wanted to be close to her. Dominique didn't want to alarm Nala more than she already had, but she knew that time meant something. Whatever 3:20 a.m. meant, Dominique hoped to be home when Nala found out.

They spoke for about a half-hour more before hanging up. She felt good about her mother agreeing to live with her. Nala was sure her other mother and father would be happy, as well. She decided to have them over one day next week for dinner to tell them.

***

By the time Pam pulled up to Nala's, it was almost 8 p.m. Nala was starting to get a little worried. She didn't want to be in the house alone for the weekend. Pam entered the house with an overnight bag, a smile and a bottle of Montoya Cabernet red wine. Nala gave her a big hug, took the bottle of wine and walked towards the kitchen. Pam followed behind her, enjoying the aroma of grilled steak, onions and green peppers. She was hungry, and the food smelled divine. Pam sat down at the kitchen table while Nala took two wine glasses from the cabinet. The table was already set for dinner. Nala popped open the bottle and poured two glasses. She sat down across from Pam and took a swallow. It tasted good as her lips puckered. She smiled and held the glass up to Pam in agreement with her choice.

"So, what's up, girl? What's going on?" Pam asked.

"I don't know. For the last two nights, *something* has been banging on my bedroom door."

Pam looked at Nala like she had lost her mind. She figured being in the house alone after a while might begin to take a toll on her, but this was way out in the left field. Pam had noticed the few times she visited Nala that she had begun to drink more. She wondered if that was contributing to her paranoia. Whatever the case, her friend needed her, and she would be there for her.

"I know it sounds crazy, and I know you think I'm crazy, but I'm not."

"Okay, okay, help me to understand. Tell me exactly what happened."

"The night before last, it took me some time to get to sleep, but I finally went. I was sleeping good, then all of a sudden, BANG, I hear on my door. I jumped up, and I'm like, what the hell is that. My heart is pounding, and it happens again, but this time it's constant. BANG, BANG, BANG!!! I'm frozen now. I'm scared. I have no gun, but I do have my metal bat by the bed. I slowly get up and grab my bat, and tiptoe to the door. BANG, BANG, BANG! My God, I'm wondering who is in my house. So, I just stand there, heart beating fast, breathing heavy, sweating and all. After a while, it gets silent. So, I open my door slowly and peek out my bedroom. I look both ways down the hall, then I leave my room and check the house. Nothing. The crazy thing is my alarm was still on."

"Wow. And the same thing happened last night too?"

"Yes. Same thing, same time. This time, it seemed like whoever was outside my door was going to get in. I was scared as hell. I called the cops, and they stayed on the phone with me until the police got to my house."

"I'm speechless. This sounds like some paranormal activity mess. You got a ghost in your house, girl?" she asked jokingly.

"Girl, I don't know. That's why I asked you to come over, so if it happens again, I have a witness."

"Well, what if it does happen again and only you can hear it?"

Nala sat, knowing that was a sure possibility. If it did happen like that, she didn't know what she was going to do. If no one else can hear it, it's still her personal mess, and she doesn't have anyone to share in it with her. Nala got up and fixed their plates of steak with onion and green pepper, garlic and cheese mashed potatoes and sautéed Brussel sprouts. Pam filled both of their glasses with more wine, and they began to eat. After dinner, they both went into the living room, and Nala turned on some music. They sat on the sofa with their legs crossed Indian style and covered themselves with the blanket. Nala refilled their glasses, and they were good. Nala thought it felt nice to have some girl company, especially Pam's. When she and Kendrick were still together, they did a lot as couples. Dinner, movies, concerts, cook-outs; you name it and they did it. Nala missed those days. Although she was done with Kendrick, that was something she enjoyed that they did together. Pam took a few sips of her wine and set her glass down on the glass end table. Nala gulped up the last of her wine and refilled her glass. Pam tried not to look at her with concern, but she was.

51

"So, besides the strange banging on your bedroom door, what else is going on with you?"

"A lot, actually. My mother, my birth mother that is, is coming here to live with me. She's been released, and I'm just waiting for them to tell me when I can go and get her."

"Oh wow! I know you're happy. How did it happen?"

"Well, I knew she was up for review for parole when I visited her. I got a phone call earlier in the week telling me she was granted release. I actually talked to her earlier and she's happy too."

"So, did you tell your mother yet? Ms. Josephine, you know who I mean."

"Not yet. I'm going to have them over probably Monday for dinner and tell them. She'll be happy too."

"I'm sure she will be. Her sister is coming home."

"Yeah, it should be a nice reunion. So, that's the good news; now for the drama."

"Oh Lord, what now?"

"Kendrick and Crystal sent the cops to my job."

"What? Why?" Pam inquired.

"Apparently, someone put a baby doll in a gift box, wrapped up nice and sat it on their porch. But the kicker is, the doll had no arms or legs, and the head was removed. They thought I did it. Is that crazy or what?"

Pam picked up her glass and took a big gulp. She remembered when Kendrick told Mike Nala was harassing them. Pam knew how much she hated them both. It didn't seem too farfetched that she might do something to piss them off. However, Pam hoped she didn't do that because that was a little deranged.

"Yeah, that is crazy. Why would they think you did it? Did someone see you?"

"No. I guess I'm supposed to be the scorned, bitter ex-wife who can't accept her husband has moved on with his mistress who is now expecting a baby."

"A baby?"

"Yes, a baby. I thought I told you."

"Maybe you did, but I forgot. So, what did the police say?"

"They just asked a bunch of questions. Detective Jackson, who was asking all the questions, is fine as hell, girl. He was sweet. Now his partner, I wanted to kick his teeth out his mouth. He was very disrespectful."

"But why would they think you did it? Because you're the ex?"

"I guess so. But like I told the cop, I wouldn't be surprised if Crystal has had a run-in with another man's wife. That seems to be her M.O. Befriend the wife, take the husband."

"That's scary, though. A package left at your door with a dismembered doll. I'd be freaking out too."

"Well, I can't say I feel sorry for her. All the dirt you do is bound to come back and bite you in the ass. She's getting whatever she dished out back."

"That may be true, but she's pregnant now. There's more at stake. The baby is innocent."

"Pam, there are always casualties of war." Nala smiled and finished her wine in her glass. She poured the remainder from the bottle in her empty glass and took another swig.

Pam felt a streak of coldness from her that made her think she was behind the incident. She loved Nala very much, but there were times she was unsure of her. Since the break-up with Kendrick, Pam had noticed a change in Nala's behavior. She drank more, and she seemed more callous at times. Pam hoped it was just a reaction from the break-up and nothing permanent.

It was almost 12:30 a.m. by the time they said their goodnights and went up to bed. Nala had Pam walk around the house with her to check and make sure all the doors and windows were locked. Before going upstairs, they both checked the alarm system and it was on. If she was awakened again, there would be someone to say everything was locked and secure. Pam had taken a hot shower before climbing into bed. She was extremely tired, but she wanted to call Mike to tell him goodnight and that she loved him. She talked to him for about twenty minutes before hanging up. She told him a little of what Nala said about the doll incident, but she didn't go into too much detail. She didn't want to be overheard by Nala, and she really wanted to get Mike's opinion once they talked about it fully. From what she did tell him, he wasn't sure what to think.

Nala was sleeping more peacefully than she had for the last two nights when the loud banging on her door began. She quickly sat up, startled by the sound, and looked at the time. The clock read 3:20 a.m. as the banging became louder and fiercer. Nala was somewhat sure no one had gotten into her house, but she couldn't say one hundred percent.

BANG, BANG, BANG, the sound roared as it ricocheted off the walls. Nala felt her body beginning to tremble as she slowly got out of her bed in fear. She picked up the metal bat and her cell phone and dialed Pam. Pam answered on the third ring, sounding groggy and raspy.

"Pam, Pam, do you hear it?" Nala whispered.

"Huh?" Pam mumbled as she tried to compose herself.

"The banging. Do you hear it? You have to hear it. It's so loud," Nala said fearfully.

Pam sat up in bed and turned on the lamp on the nightstand. She could hear how scared Nala was. Pam was fully alert by now as she got up and walked slowly to the door. She could hear nothing, but she waited to see if the banging would happen again so that she would hear it. "I don't hear anything. I'm walking to the door to look out."

"No, Pam, be careful! Let's just call the police again," Nala frantically said.

"It's okay, Nala. I'm coming to you."

Pam slowly opened the door and looked down the hall. There was no one there, but she could still hear Nala asking, "Do you hear it?" Pam walked to Nala's door and called her name.

"Pam is that you?" she asked, moving apprehensively toward the door.

"Yeah, it's me. Open up."

Nala quickly ran to the door and opened it. She had the metal bat in one hand and her cellphone in the other. Pam walked in and could see how terrified she was. She led Nala back to her bed, so she could sit down. Pam went into her bathroom and got a glass of water. She gave it to Nala, and she drank a few sips. Nala thought to herself that a glass of wine would be better at a time like this.

"Please tell me you heard it?" Nala asked, hoping she could truly share in her fear.

"I didn't, sorry. Maybe it's a bad dream you're having."

"No, it's not Pam!" she said with frustration. "For the last three nights, there has been banging on my bedroom door at 3:20 in the morning. Why? What is going on?" she asked, beginning to cry.

Pam sat next to her on the bed and hugged her. She didn't know what was happening, but, whatever the case, it was real to her friend. She hated seeing her that way. Nala wasn't weak in any sense of the word, but whatever was going on had her completely vulnerable. Pam went back into the bathroom and got a sleeping pill from the cabinet. She gave it to Nala and helped her lie down. Nala smiled at her friend, thankful she was there.

"I didn't mean to yell at you."

"It's okay. Listen, I'm going to stay in here with you. You get some sleep and we'll talk in the morning. Okay?"

"Okay. Thanks, Pam."

Pam climbed on the other side of the king bed and covered up under the quilt. Before long, they were both asleep.

# Chapter 6

Nala was still asleep when Pam got up. She went downstairs and put on a pot of coffee. She figured Nala would be getting up soon and coffee would be a good thing. Pam still wasn't sure of what to make of the night before. She heard nothing, but clearly Nala did. Pam didn't believe in ghosts or paranormal stuff, but something was evidently happening. Nala was a rational woman, and for her to believe she heard something made Pam think of other possibilities, no matter how strange it sounded.

Pam was watching the news when Nala came downstairs. She walked into the kitchen with a forced smile. She couldn't seem to make eye contact with Pam because she was embarrassed. She didn't know what Pam was thinking of her. Nala sat at the table while Pam poured her a cup of coffee. She sat it in front of her as Nala prepared it to her liking. There was an awkward silence while they both sipped their hot drinks. Nala would catch a glimpse of Pam while she wasn't looking. She was trying to read where her head was.

"So, how did you sleep?" Pam asked, breaking the silence.

"I slept good."

"That's good. Are you hungry? I can fix something if you want."

"No, I'm good right now. This coffee is just what I needed."

As they drank their coffee, Nala sat her cup down on the table hard and turned to the TV. The news commenter caught her attention with the story she was reporting. She grabbed the remote and turned it up louder.

"It was a full house as notorious serial killer Robert Randstad was executed in the facility where he spent the last years of his life on death row. Randstad was tried and convicted for the brutal murders of seven women. Many family members of the victims were there to witness the execution, as well as protestors outside the prison opposing the execution. It was reported that Randstad looked at peace when asked if he had any final words. He said, "I was doing God's work, and I will be rewarded in death. Nothing is ever final." Randstad was pronounced dead at 3:20 a.m."

Pam looked at Nala as her eyes widened like saucers. Her mother's words rang loud in her ear concerning the significance of the time. 3:20 a.m. did mean something just as she said. Nala had forgotten about Randstad's execution. With the strange things going on in her home and Crystal and Kendrick sending the police to her job, he was the last thing on her mind. Nala sat silently for a few minutes. She knew the day would come for him to be executed, but now that it had come and gone, she didn't know what to feel. After all, he was a serial killer, a sociopath, a cold-blooded murderer. If there was anything to feel, it should be for his victims.

Nala wanted a drink badly, but she didn't know how that would look to Pam with it being so early in the morning. But she craved it. She needed to taste the first sweetness of it that warmed her entire body. Nala got up and left out of the kitchen. When she returned, she had a bottle of wine. She tried not to look at Pam as she went to the cabinet and took out a glass. She filled it to the top, mumbled something under her breath, raised her glass and then drank most of it. When she lowered the glass, Pam was looking at her with an awkward expression on her face. At that point, Nala didn't care. She began to feel the warmness take over her, and it felt good.

"I needed that," she said, sitting back down. "The coffee wasn't strong enough for a moment like this."

"So, how do you feel?" asked Pam.

"Um, fine. I mean, everyone knew it was coming. He deserved to be killed. Bottom line."

"Yeah, well, I'm swayed on the death penalty. Too many innocent people have gone to the electric chair. When you don't get it right, I have a problem."

"Well, believe me, they got it right this time," she said, finishing the wine in her glass.

"So, Nala, how's the case going in Philly with the murders there? Haven't heard too much about it from you?"

"They still have a killer on their hands. But, as serial killers do, he or she is taking a break or as we call it, a 'cooling-off period.'"

"And why do they take breaks? Are they tired, remorseful, or just plotting out their next strategies for their next kills?"

"It's different for some, so I can't definitely say."

"Well, just for speculation, why do you think this killer is taking a break?"

"Speculation, right?"

"Mmm-hmmm."

"I think they're just waiting for the next opportunity to do what they do. I'm sure if another unsuspecting victim goes into their radar, they will kill him on the spot."

"Wow, that's just so cold-hearted."

"And so is cheating on your wife."

Pam looked at Nala and gave her a half-smile. She filled her glass half full and drank the wine in her glass. Pam tried not to look too concerned, but she was. Of all the years they had been friends, she never witnessed Nala drinking as much as she did now. Pam didn't think she was an alcoholic, but, at the rate she was going, it wouldn't take long.

Pam got up and started to clean off the table, so she could put the dishes in the dishwasher. Nala tried to help, but Pam insisted she relax. Nala was glad Pam was there, and she was glad she was such a good friend. The only thing that was really keeping her sane was her job, family and Pam. After Pam finished cleaning the kitchen, they went into the living room to watch TV. Before long, they were both asleep on the couch.

Nala and Pam hadn't realized how tired they were. When they finally awoke from their nap, it was almost 3:00 in the afternoon. They both sat up and rushed for the bathroom. When Pam finished, she walked over to Nala's room and sat on the bed, waiting for her to come out of the bathroom.

"I guess we were tired, huh," Nala said, plopping down on the bed next to Pam.

"Yeah, I guess so."

"So, how about I take you out for some dinner and drinks later? What do you have a taste for?"

"You know what, some Indian food sounds good."

"I know of a place on Walnut St. in Philly called Masal Kitchen. The food is really good. So okay, Indian food it is. And before dinner, some shopping. I need a few things. The weather will be breaking soon, and I need to add some Spring clothes to my collection and maybe a few more Winter items. Okay, so let's get ourselves together and head out."

"Sounds like a plan."

***

Nala and Pam had driven to a few boutiques on the main line and found some really good items. A few things turned into three bags of clothes each, with two extra bags of shoes. They felt like kids in a candy store and couldn't resist buying most of what they liked. By the time they were finished, they both had worked up a hearty appetite. Nala lucked up and found a parking spot on the same street as the restaurant. With it being a Saturday, she was surprised. The two went in and found a seat next to the window. There was a nice crowd inside, and the atmosphere was nice. Pam and Nala looked over the menu, quickly choosing what they wanted. They were both hungry and ready to eat. The waitress, a friendly, bubbly, young, white girl, sat a glass of water in front of each of them and pulled her pad and pen out her shirt pocket.

"Are you ready to order?" she politely asked.

"Yes. I'll start with the mixed veggie rolls. Do you want to share, or you're getting your own appetizer?" asked Nala.

"We can share," Pam said with a smile.

"Okay, so the veggie rolls to start. Then, I'll have the Chicken Biryani Platter and a Mango Lassi.

"Okay. And ma'am, what would you like?"

"I'll have the Chicken and Lamb platter with a Kala Khatta."

"Great. I'll bring your drinks shortly."

"Thank you," they both said.

As Nala and Pam sat waiting for their drinks to be brought to them, Nala noticed a man and woman who had entered. What brought attention to them was the way the man was staring at her. They looked to be a couple, so he was already off-limits to her. As the woman was about to sit down, which would have made her face Nala, the man quickly moved her to the other chair. The woman smiled, having no clue her man was setting up his flirt game. He sat down without pulling out her seat and gave Nala a smile. Nala smiled back and continued her conversation with Pam. The waitress returned with their drinks and appetizers, then went to the table with the man and woman. Nala could feel him looking at her every now and then as she looked up from eating her veggie rolls.

The waitress left their table and walked to the back. It was evident how much the woman loved her man. She kept trying to hold his hand and be affectionate, but he wasn't returning the gestures. She just smiled and kept loving on him while he was lusting on Nala. He was beginning to agitate Nala. He was completely disregarding his woman. Nala was curious to know if they were married, but she didn't know how to find out. Just as she was trying to figure it out, another couple entered. To the man's surprise, he was taken off guard by the two people being there.

"Surprise!" the woman said as the man stood up, shook the other man's hand, and hugged the girl. "I wanted them to surprise you for our wedding anniversary," she said loudly, proudly and happily. She opened her arms, reached for her husband, and gave him a kiss.

After they all sat down, he continued to give Nala the interested eye while his wife smiled and enjoyed being his wife. Nala was disgusted at how disrespectful he was. The waitress brought their food, and she tried not to pay him any mind as she and Pam talked and ate. However, she knew what type of man he was. One way or another, he was going to approach her.

"This is really good," said Pam.

"Yeah, they have good food here, and the prices are reasonable. But girl, check this out. Dude behind you at the table has been eyeing me since he and his wife got in here."

"Who? The one whose wife surprised him?"

"Yes. He's so busy looking at me he can't even enjoy what his wife is trying to do for him. You see, he's the type of brother who gets his balls cut off because he's slimy."

"Yeah, well, we know it's in some of their nature. We shouldn't even be surprised at how some men act and treat their wives." After Pam made the comment, she felt bad because that was Nala's story. Pam at one time thought Kendrick was a good, faithful husband who adored Nala, but after she found out about his infidelity, she viewed him totally different. "I'm sorry, I didn't...."

"Girl, please. My husband was a low-life cheating bastard who did me wrong. Just like that man is doing his wife. You know what, watch this. I'm going to show you how men ain't shit."

"What are you going to do?" Pam said curiously as Nala stood up and walked over to the table.

The man almost choked on his drink as he saw Nala approaching the table. She had to admit he was fine, but all the good looks made him look like a monster for how he was treating his wife behind her back. When Nala reached the table, the man's wife looked up at her with a surprised look as she wiped her mouth and smiled.

"I don't mean to impose, but I heard you say this was your wedding anniversary. I just wanted to say congratulations and many happier years."

"Oh, thank you so much," the wife said, standing up and giving her a hug. "Wasn't that nice of her, hun?"

"Yeah, it was. Thank you."

"Well, I'll let you good folks get back to dinner. Once again, congratulations."

Nala walked away as the man stood up to show a sign of respect for her. That was more than he had done for his wife. Nala sat back down to Pam smiling and shaking her head. The man looked at Nala with even more lust for her. That had completely turned him on. Now, he was trying to figure out how to get her.

Pam and Nala had finished their food and were waiting for the waitress to bring the check and their doggie bags. Nala had an idea on how to bait the man, so she left her credit card to pay the bill and excused herself to go to the bathroom. She could see the man watching her as she got up, then she felt his gaze burning her back as she walked away. Knowing within time he would follow, Nala went into the bathroom, freshened her lips, powdered her face a little, and then waited. After about five minutes, she opened the door, and there he stood, waiting like a piranha.

"Oh, hey," she said, dumbfounded. "You had to tinkle too, huh?"

"Yeah, something like that. Listen, that was really nice of you to wish us a happy anniversary."

"Oh, no problem. You guys seem so happy. How could I not?" she said smiling.

"Yeah, well, she may be, but...."

"Oh, come on. You are too."

"What is your name?" he asked, moving closer to her.

"Dominique."

"Pretty name for a pretty woman. Mine is Bryce. Listen, I have to get back to the wifey, and I know you need to get back to your friend. Is there any way we could resume this conversation by phone, perhaps?"

"Really? You're asking me for my number, and upstairs you have an excited wife who obviously adores you and is celebrating your wedding anniversary? Now, how cold is that?"

"It's a long story, but in a nutshell, it's been cold for a long time. Look, I'm not a monster or a dog, but things are complicated right now."

"And asking another woman for her number wouldn't complicate it anymore"?

"No, it wouldn't. Trust me."

Nala's blood boiled as the lies spewed from his mouth. To make matters even worse, he had the audacity to ask her to trust him. How is a woman supposed to trust a man who's trying to cheat on his wife with her? Trust was already a phantom when he approached her. However, she would play his game.

"Okay, you have a phone?"

"Sure do," he said, quickly removing it from his pants pocket.

Nala took it from his hand and entered her number. If he could have fucked her right then and there, he would have. Nala was so disgusted with him she tried not to touch his hand when handing him back his phone. But of course, he couldn't resist, and he rubbed his hand over hers.

"I bet the rest of you is soft, just like your hands."

"Maybe."

"Okay, so I'll call you tonight when things settle down at home."

"No, you can call tomorrow. It's your anniversary. Your wife at least deserves your attention for today."

"And she has it. I just thought we could talk more in detail, you know."

"And we will, but tomorrow. Look, I have to go."

"Okay, well, I'll call you tomorrow. Now, don't stand a brother up by not answering your phone."

"If I was going to do that, I wouldn't have given you my number. Enjoy the rest of your day Bryce."

Nala brushed by him and went back upstairs to the restaurant. The bill had been paid, and their bags were packed. Nala slipped on her coat as Bryce came from downstairs. He walked past her and went to sit back down. His wife gave him a big smile as she leaned forward, giving him a taste of the cake their friends had brought. Nala could tell she was madly in love with him. She felt sorry she didn't know she was married to a scum bag. As Nala and Pam walked past their table, Nala stopped and congratulated them once more. The wife was extremely happy as she thanked her and offered them some cake. They both declined and left.

*\*\**

Nala didn't tell Pam about her encounter with Bryce down by the bathroom because she knew what she planned to do. After they looked at their clothes and shoes again and drank wine in the living room while listening to a 70's old school, slow jams, mixed tape, they both went up to bed. Pam offered to sleep in the room with Nala, but she said no. Nala knew the banging would stop because Randstad was dead. For some reason, he was preparing her for his death. Nala remembered she was supposed to receive a package from him after his execution. Hopefully, that would explain a lot of what was going on. Nala snuggled under the covers and began to feel herself dozing. As she positioned herself in bed to welcome sleep, her cell phone started to buzz. Nala wondered if the banging would be replaced with her cell phone buzzing. She looked at the time. It was 12:15 a.m. Nala picked up the phone, and, to her surprise, it was Bryce.

"Hello," she sleepily said.

"Hey, I know it's late, but I wanted to see how you were doing."

"Uh, it's after 12 am and I'm sleep. I asked you to call me tomorrow."

"Well, technically, it is tomorrow, right?"

"Listen, shouldn't you be somewhere making love to your wife?"

"No. It's complicated."

"Hmmm, that's what you all say. Look, it's late. I'm tired and ready to go back to sleep."

"Okay, okay, I'm not trying to mess up before we even get started. I apologize for calling you so late. I'll call you later today."

"When the sun rises and beyond. Not too early, please."

"Well, so that I won't mess up again, what's a good time to call?"

"My girl and I are still having our girls' weekend, so call later in the evening, around 8. I should be free then."

"Okay, 8 it is. You sleep well, precious, and I'll talk to you later."

"Yeah, okay. Goodnight."

Nala ended the call and felt like she was going to throw up. She hated the sound of his voice. She hated even more that he called her precious. That sounded so cheap to her. Nala thought back to when she told Pam about serial killers having a cooling-off period. Well, she felt she was cooled off enough. Bryce was about to bring her back into commission.

## Chapter 7

Nala and Pam went to breakfast before Pam headed out. She wanted to get back to Jersey before Mike got home from his weekend. Nala felt good now. She knew the banging would stop and life would go on, that was until the mysterious package from Randstad arrived. For now, she would just take it one day at a time. When she got back to the house, she went into her office and checked her email. She was hoping to hear when she could go and get her mother, Dominique. With excitement, she saw an email pertaining to that, and she quickly opened it up. The email stated she could personally pick up her mother next Sunday. Nala smiled and immediately booked a round-trip flight to California. The facility where her mother was staying had taken care of her airfare. Nala knew she had to tell her parents now. There was no more time left. Next week, her biological mother would be home. Nala picked up her cell phone and dialed her mom. She would invite them over to dinner on Monday, but she figured she may have to do it today. This week would be busy with getting things ready for Dominique. The phone rang three times before her mother answered. Nala didn't know why she was so nervous. After all, shouldn't her mother be thrilled to see her sister home?

"Hey, mom, how are you?"

"Hey, hon. Wow, haven't talked to you in quite some time. How are you?"

"Oh, busy, busy, busy. Work, cases, life, you know. How's dad?"

"He's good. He just asked me yesterday when was the last time I spoke to you. I was going to call you today myself."

"Great minds think alike, huh? Listen, Mom, are you and dad busy later today?"

"No, not really. Why? What's up?"

"I wanted to invite you guys to dinner. Like you said, we haven't seen each other in a while, so I thought it would be nice."

"Yeah, we can do that. That would be nice."

"Good. And bring an overnight bag, so y'all won't have to drive back tonight. Y'all can leave tomorrow or whenever. I do have to work, but you can stay for as long as you want."

"Oh, okay. Well, we'll leave tomorrow. Your dad has a doctor's appointment on Tuesday. So, ok, well, it sounds like a plan."

"Okay, Mom, then I'll see you later. Love you."

"Love you too."

Nala got up and went into the kitchen and opened her freezer. She took out a roast beef to make for dinner. She would add vegetables and gravy and put it in the crockpot to simmer for the day. Afterward, she got a glass from the cabinet and the bottle of wine she and Pam hadn't finished. Nala went upstairs and ran her a hot bubble bath. She turned on some jazz and slid in the tub as it filled with hot water. Nala poured herself a glass of wine and took a sip before setting it down on the tub. She closed her eyes and thought about what the week was going to bring.

\*\*\*

The house was smelling of good Sunday food when Nala's parents arrived. She met them at the door and gave each of them a big hug. Nala was glad to see them. Having them stay over would be wonderful. They both entered the house, and Nala took their bag and headed into the living room as they followed. She turned on the TV and handed her dad the remote. He was in heaven. Nala didn't know if she should wait until dinner to tell them the news or just do it now and get it over with. She decided to wait until dinner. Nala and her mother went into the kitchen while she checked on the food. Dinner was ready, so it was up to them when they would eat.

"So, how have you been?" asked her mother.

"I'm okay. Like I said earlier, just working," she responded while setting the table.

"You look good."

"Awww, thanks. I try," Nala said, laughing.

"So, have you heard from Kendrick?"

"Uh, yeah. It's a long story, one of which I don't want to get into and spoil the day."

"What happened?" she asked curiously with concern.

Nala really didn't want to have any type of conversation that pertained to Kendrick. It was enough she was telling them her mother was coming to live with her. She didn't want to add to the load by telling her Kendrick and his home-wrecker sent the cops to her job. However, she couldn't wait to tell Dominique. She knew she would understand why Nala sent the doll. She couldn't tell her other mother that. She just wouldn't understand.

"Nothing much. He just sent the police to my job because he thought I sent a cut-up doll baby to his house."

"What? Why would he think that?"

"I don't know, Mom. He's crazy; she's crazy."

"Well, what did the police say?"

"Not too much. It was actually all formalities, that's all. They got a complaint, so they had to investigate. Nothing came out of it. Everything is fine."

"Oh, my goodness. I'm so done with that man. I thought he was so much better than this. He had us all fooled, huh?"

"Yeah, well, don't let it spoil our day."

"How's the divorce coming along? Papers signed on both ends?"

"Yes, but it's not that simple."

"Well, how..."

"Mom," Nala interrupted. "We're not talking about Kendrick today. Okay? I actually have something else to talk to you and dad about. Are you guys ready to eat?"

"What do you have to talk about? Is everything okay?"

"Mom, go and get dad and we'll talk," she said, shaking her head.

Nala sat the food on the table and waited for her parents to come back into the kitchen. Her roast beef and vegetables looked good, along with the greens and red potatoes. Nala sat the corn muffins on the table and sat down. Her parents entered the kitchen and smiled as they looked at the food.

"Daddy, can you say grace please?"

"Sure, sweetheart."

Nala extended her hands, and they held each other's hand while her father prayed. Afterward, they began to fix their plates.

"Mmmm," Nala's mother said as she tasted the roast beef.

Nala smiled and began to eat.

"So Nala, you said you wanted to talk to us. What's up?"

"Well, Mom and Dad, I have some news I think is good news and you both will be glad to hear."

"What is it? You can't be pregnant, thanks to Kendrick, so what is it?"

"Mom is coming to live with me. I go and pick her up on Sunday."

Nala's parents looked at each other in shock. She wasn't sure how she should take their reaction. Was it a good shock or a bad shock? Nala sat waiting to see which one as her parents continued to look surprised.

"What? How? How is that possible?" asked her mother.

"Well, you remember when I went out there to visit she told me her review was coming up. They did the review, and she was granted release. A lot more happened to help that, but the bottom line is she's coming home. Isn't that great?"

"Yes, baby, it is." Her mother's voice cracked. "I haven't seen my sister in over thirty years. That's how she wanted it. This is wonderful news!"

Nala was overjoyed that her mother was happy. It made her mother's return all the sweeter. After dinner,

Nala's father went into the movie room to watch a movie while Nala and her mother talked more about Dominique's return. Nala could sense her mother was legitimately happy, but for some reason, she sensed something else. She didn't know if it was nervousness or shock, but it was something. Nala would make it her business to ensure her mother and father continued to feel loved and appreciated. After all, they were a big part of her success. She owed them her gratitude and respect.

On the other hand, Dominique harbored the same demons she did regarding murder. That connection was deeply rooted between the two of them, even though they had just become a part of each other's lives. Whatever the case, she was coming home, and Nala was ecstatic.

*** 

Crystal was feeling sick to her stomach when she woke up. She turned to the other side of the bed, and Kendrick was not there. She looked at the clock. It was going on six in the evening. She wondered had she slept that long as she sat up in bed. The house was really quiet as Crystal got up and walked out of the bedroom.

"Kendrick," she called as she leaned over the banister looking downstairs.

There was no response.

Crystal walked slowly down the stairs while rubbing her stomach. She figured she would drink a warm glass of milk in hopes that it would make her feel better. When she got downstairs, the house was dark, minus the light in the kitchen. Kendrick was nowhere to be found.

Crystal warmed up her milk and headed back upstairs. She sat down on the bed and reached for her cellphone, which was on the nightstand. There were no missed calls or text messages from Kendrick. Crystal drank some of her milk then dialed his number. It immediately went to voicemail. Now very curious about where he was with his phone off, she drank the rest of her milk and wondered.

No stranger to the game, she knew what a turned-off cell could mean. Although Kendrick tried to act supportive and loving, at times, she could sense his coldness. She felt like his affection was forced sometimes. It worried her because she knew how that chick Karma could be. After all, look how she got him. She turned on the TV and laid back down. Eventually, he would come home. Then, he would have some explaining to do.

## Chapter 8

Nala felt good about her visit with her parents and the sharing of the news about her mother. Her parents had left pretty early in the morning. They wanted to beat the morning rush hour. When she got to work that morning, she fixed herself a cup of coffee and sat behind her desk. She was leaving for California on Friday, so she wanted to make sure she had everything done. Nala began checking her email and noticed she had a message from Detective Chase. He was asking to meet with her concerning the case. Nala had been brushing him off lately, so she knew she would eventually have to meet with him. She responded and set up an appointment for Wednesday. As she continued perusing her messages, her cell phone rang. She looked at the number and noticed it was Bryce. Nala took a deep breath, rolled her eyes and answered. She figured if she didn't answer, he would continue to call.

"Yes, hello."

"Good morning, Dominique. How are you?"

"I'm good. Just going over some things before my day begins."

"Oh, okay. I didn't get a chance to call you yesterday, so I said I better do it today. Don't want to be too much out of sight, then I'd be out of mind. So, what kind of work do you do?" he asked curiously.

"I'm an entrepreneur."

"Okay, so what do you exactly do?"

"I have my own cleaning business. I get rid of stuff people don't want or need."

"That's what's up. Hey, uh, listen. I'm trying to see you. I want to take you out. Are you busy tonight?"

"Actually, I am. But I have a question."

"Shoot."

"The other day, when you stalked me by the bathroom, you said your marriage is complicated. Why is that? Your wife seems like a sweetheart."

"Yeah, she is. She's a really good woman, but we weren't supposed to get married. Listen. It's a long story."

"I have a little time." Nala wanted to see what lies he would tell to justify stepping out on his wife. She wanted to know every little detail. The more she despised him, the easier it would be to cut him up. She could smell the bullshit seeping through the phone. It stunk bad.

"Alright. We got married about three years ago after I found out she was pregnant. She cried and begged me to marry her because her family was really religious, and her being pregnant would be a major disaster for her if she had no husband."

"Really? Are you serious? Do you know how many men get women pregnant and don't marry them? Hell, some of them don't even take care of the child. Nooo, there is more to this story. You don't seem like the type to be bullied or coerced into something you don't want to do. So what's the real deal?"

"Damn, you're good. Well, her family has some really nice money. And..."

"Say no more."

"So, you think I ain't shit now, right? Excuse my language.

"I'm not going to judge. You do what you have to do."

"Okay, so can I see you?"

"Not tonight. But maybe Wednesday. I'll call you. Now I have to go."

"Okay, cool. Don't forget to call me," he excitedly said.

"Oh no, I won't. We'll definitely hook up."

Nala ended the call and placed the phone down with a disgusted look on her face. She was definitely going to rid the world of that scum bag. Nala gathered her belongings and went into the classroom. She was interested to hear how the students progressed on their cases, especially Jessica. Nala stood in front of her desk as the students entered the classroom. They all sat down, eager to begin. Before beginning class, Nala stood observing the students for a moment. She wanted to get a feel of them through their expressions. All she saw from them was a fire and tenacity for what they were doing. That was the look she wanted to see.

"So, you've had the weekend to review your cases. Everything you need to profile the perp was in your folder. I'm eager to hear what you have compiled. Shall we begin?"

***

Crystal had awakened early that morning, hoping to speak with Kendrick about his whereabouts from yesterday, but he was already gone. When she arrived at work, she got the coffee started and checked her emails. She wanted to make sure she had nothing pressing to do before the head of her department arrived. Crystal locked her office and headed over to the other side of campus to see Kendrick. He looked to be working hard when she knocked on his office door and walked inside. Crystal couldn't tell what expression his face read. Was it, "I'm busted," "Why is she here?" or "Glad to see her?" She walked over to the chair in front of his desk and placed her hand on it while the other was on her hip. He knew she was pissed, and the majority of him didn't care.

"I was hoping to catch you this morning since I didn't see you last night. Where did you disappear too?"

"I didn't disappear. I just left. You were sleeping so good I didn't want to wake you, so I didn't."

"Well, why didn't you leave me a note or call? I called you, and your phone went straight to voicemail. What was that all about?"

Kendrick chuckled as he sat back in his chair, looking at her. He was reminded of something Nala said about Crystal having the looks but lacking the brains. She was definitely fine, and her sex game was on point, but she couldn't hold a light to Nala when it came to intelligence. That was what he missed about her. She was the complete package. Beautiful, smart, intelligent, articulate and freaky. Kendrick missed the conversations they had about school policy, the government and things that mattered. He couldn't go that deep with Crystal. She tried to at times, and all it did was make her sound like a dumb Becky.

"Do you realize that I am working tirelessly on the curriculum changes? We are in the final stretch, and it's extremely busy and crucial to our success right now. I was here yesterday until God knows when. I went home, slept for a few hours then got right back at it. If you paid some attention to what I'm doing, then you wouldn't have to ask questions."

"Oh, so now I don't pay attention? I'm fully aware of what you're doing. Hell, I've even typed several things for you. It would just be nice if I could get a common courtesy call when you're going to be gone for a long time."

"Are we adults or children here? I wasn't thinking about calling because I was knee-deep in work and calling to check in wasn't a priority. I didn't have to worry about this with Nala," he said under his breath.

Crystal gasped and stepped back, looking angrily at Kendrick. There it was. There were his true feelings being revealed. After the last time, she thought he hadn't gotten over Nala, but he assured her he had that it was over. She realized how wrong she was. Once again, the man she felt would be her knight in shining armor showed he wasn't. That was the story of her life. Her mother was right about her and men. She gave too easily and fell too hard. In the end, she was always the one getting burned.

"You didn't have to worry about what with Nala?"

"Being questioned like I'm a kid. I don't have time for this, Crystal. I got too much to do. Why are you trying to throw me off my mark?"

"Don't turn this around on me. All I wanted to know was where you were and why your phone was off. Is that too much to ask? We're in a relationship. That means we communicate with one another. It's not about checking in. It's called common courtesy!"

"Crystal, I hear you, but not now. I have a meeting in an hour and a half. I need to be ready. I need to sound like I know what I'm talking about. This shit right here is not helping. When my meeting is over, I'll come to your office. But right now, you have to go."

Crystal stood looking at Kendrick, not knowing what to do. She wanted to curse him out for what he said about Nala, but she didn't want to continue to take him off his mark. She decided to go the high road and leave it alone until his meeting was over. But once it was clear to go in, she would go all the way in, no punches held.

"Okay, Kendrick. I'll be waiting for you when you're done."

Crystal turned and walked away, not giving him room to respond. She closed the door behind her as Kendrick tried to regroup. His intentions weren't to hurt Crystal, but because whatever little affection or lust he had for her was leaving quickly, his true image showed.

***

When Crystal got back to her office, she took an orange juice from the refrigerator and sat behind her desk. Her boss had already arrived, and Crystal knew she needed to regroup and quickly. She took a deep breath and put on her game face. Crystal buzzed her boss to say good morning and to ask if she was needed. She was told she would have to take some shorthand within an hour, so a letter could be sent out by early afternoon to the rest of the department. As Crystal began resuming her work from yesterday, she tried to focus, but it was hard. This entire situation reminded her of Warren. Crystal picked up her cell and dialed her mother. She rubbed her stomach as she felt the movement of her world inside of her.

"Hey baby, is everything okay?" her mother asked with concern.

There was a pause before Crystal answered, "I don't know."

"What's wrong?"

"It's Kendrick. I don't know what's up with him. One minute I'm the love of his life, and the next, I feel like a stranger on the street."

"Since you called me, then you want my opinion or advice, right?"

"That's fine, but I don't want your judgment."

"You're pregnant, and there's nothing you can do about that now. However, you don't need to stay with him because of that. Pack up, come home, and we'll deal with it."

"But I don't want to come home, Mom. I love him, and I want to be here, with my baby."

"Oh child, when are you going to learn? You said the same thing about Warren, and where did that get you? A restraining order against you and thirty days in jail. These men don't care nothing about you. All they want is to screw you and drop you like trash. This Kendrick guy is no different. You were fun in the beginning. Sex every day, all day. The thrill and excitement of not getting caught while cheating. Girl, you were a rollercoaster ride for him, but now all that's been taken away. You're not the side piece that he can play with when he feels like it anymore. You're the main course, and it was never supposed to be that way. Crystal, you need to run for the hills before you get so hurt there's no turning back."

"No, I'm not doing that. Kendrick is nothing like Warren."

"Really? Okay, Crystal, you got it. I'll just be here when it all goes to hell like I always am. I love you very much, and I'm tired of seeing you make the same mistakes. You have to change. You have to do different."

"Okay, yeah, mom, I hear you. Well, I have to go—duty calls. I'll call you later in the week. Bye."

Crystal ended the call before her mother started up again. She knew she was right, but she didn't want to hear it. She preferred hearing how much her mother loved her and that everything would be all right. However, Crystal never knew her mother to take the subtle route with anything. Crystal felt she needed to regain her position with Kendrick if she was to be his wife.

*** 

After class was over, Jessica gathered her belongings and rushed towards Nala. Nala figured she would have questions, so she took her time putting her things in her briefcase. Jessica waited for the rest of the students to leave before she walked over to her.

"Excuse me, Dr. Jordan, but do you have a minute?"

"That's about all I have. We can walk and talk," she said, leaving the classroom.

"Okay, I was reading over the case notes, your profile, and I looked at all the crime scene photos. I'm just wondering why this unsub has taken a hiatus."

"There could be many reasons. Give me a few?"

"Well, something could have changed in their life. Um, they could have relocated, or they could have died. Been caught on another charge."

"Okay. So, out of the examples you just gave, which one do you think applies to your killer?"

"I would say something has changed in their life."

"So now, you have to go through all the evidence you have and figure out what you think may have changed in her life. You have to look at the case through the eyes of the killer, not the victim. What is she telling you? What is she showing you?" Question, do you think she's done?"

"No."

"Why?"

"Because I believe she enjoys killing."

"Mmmm Hmmm. Okay, Jessica, I have to go now. Just remember, you're looking through the killer's eyes and not the victim's eyes."

"Alright, thanks."

Nala went into her office and closed the door. Jessica turned and walked away with more of a zeal to help solve the case. She thought to herself how this could be a career booster if she snagged the unsub. She would feel like Clarisse Starling from "The Silence of the Lambs." Although she wasn't in the FBI Academy, she was in grad school getting her degree in criminal psychology. Helping to solve the case would put her in a totally different bracket. Jessica told herself she would do any and everything to bring Philly's most recent serial killer to justice.

## Chapter 9

Today was the day Nala was going into Philly to meet with Detective Chase. This was also the day she said she would meet up with the lying scumbag, Bryce. He had called her three times the night before to see if she was still going to meet with him. She thought that she needed to get rid of him, if only for being a pest. Nala hadn't had the luxury of killing anyone in a while. She was starting to crave it. She missed the adrenaline rush it gave her. Nala knew killing was morally wrong, but she felt God should make exceptions. Killing should not be a sin if you kill a child molester, old person, or a cheating husband. She was fully aware that her heaven card had been revoked. However, she would proudly take a seat in hell for the work she was doing.

Nala knew her visit with Detective Chase wouldn't be long. She needed to get back home and start to pack for her weekend trip to L.A. She was going to pick up her mother, Dominique, and she was excited. They hadn't spoken in a few days, and she was eager to see and talk to her. There was so much to talk about. Nala was eager to find out the shady things that were going on at the Roger Thurstman Mental Facility where she stayed. She knew there was something not right about Dr. Jacobs, and she was right. *How can you run a brothel from a mental facility?* Nala thought to herself as she chuckled. Whatever the case, she was going to jail, and her mother was coming home.

Nala got off the elevator and headed to Detective Chase's office. As she walked in there, she slowly stopped by a room with the door opened and looked inside. There she saw her work being displayed as if she were an artist at an art gallery. Crime scene photos covered the wall with different color sticky notes and push pins. Nala walked inside and stared at the wall. She couldn't believe the gruesomeness of some of her killings. "Wow, I did that, huh?" she mumbled as she smiled. Nala hadn't remembered what the photos looked like because she hadn't seen them in a while. Looking at them was like looking at them for the first time. It was exhilarating!

"Oh, there you are," Detective Chase said as he entered the room. Nala turned around and extended her hand to him to shake. "Please sit," he said, pulling out a chair at the table. He handed her a folder that she opened and began looking at its contents. It appeared they were working extensively without her. They had followed up on many leads, which led to dead ends. Nala was impressed. They wanted her badly.

"So, Dr. Jordan. What is going on? She hasn't killed in about a month. Is it safe to say she's done?"

"As I told you before, most serial killers have a cooling down period. This could be hers. I can't give you an exact science to say when she will start killing again or if she'll start killing again. It's just one of those unfortunate things you have to wait on."

"She killed a cop! I don't want to wait. I want her now."

Nala knew how much of a toll this was taking on him, and honestly, she didn't care. She was sure everyone knew about Lieutenant Frisco's extramarital affairs. They probably laughed and joked about it in the locker room. That was how men did it. It was the exclusive club most of them belonged to. If Nala had it her way, she wanted to dismantle it.

"I know you're angry and impatient, but I really don't know what else to tell you."

"Well, that student, uh… What's her name? The young lady from your class?"

"Jessica."

"Yes, Jessica. Is she helping out?"

"Actually, she is. I have a core group of students working on various cases, and she has been assigned to this case."

"Okay. The more, the merrier. Listen, Dr. Jordan, you have been a tremendous help. The department is grateful for your help and expertise. I just want this person caught. She killed innocent men and a cop. She has to be stopped."

"Innocent? Well, with all due respect, sir, these men were no saints. All of them were cheating on their wives and being dishonest. I wouldn't go as far as to give them a saint badge," she said with a chuckle.

Detective Chase looked at her with a shocked looked on his face. He was aware of the background of the men murdered but killing them was no solution. Whatever the case, he wanted to catch his killer. He didn't want this case to become a cold case and go unsolved. To avenge his friend, he had to find his murderer.

"Whatever their personal lifestyle entailed, it didn't warrant them being killed. So, what do we do now?"

"We wait. Believe me, you'll get a break. Listen, I'll take this with me and go through them again. Maybe I missed something. If I feel a new profile is needed, then I will compile it. How's that?"

"Oh, oh, that's great. Thank you. Anything you can find will help."

"No problem. Well, I must go. I'm going out of town for the weekend and need to prepare. I'll try to get back to you by the end of next week."

"Okay. Thanks again. I look forward to hearing from you next week.

"Sure."

Nala put on her coat and shades and left out of the office. She could feel her cellphone vibrating in her pocketbook, so she reached in and took it out. She let out a disgusted sigh when she saw she had four missed calls from Bryce. She couldn't wait to put him out of his misery later tonight. He was a pain in the ass, and she was sure she would be helping his wife out once she slit his throat.

When Nala got into her car, she sat for a while, contemplating if she should call him. Tonight was the night they were to meet, and Detective Chase did want another break in the case. Nala dialed his number and tapped her manicured nails on the steering wheel. When he answered, the sound of his voice irritated her immensely.

"Hey, lady. Glad you called me back."

"Well, you did call four times. What's up?"

"I'm just confirming tonight. We're still on, right?"

"Yeah. Where are we meeting?"

"Do you like Greek food?"

"Absolutely."

"Well, there is this place down on Locust Street called Estia Restaurant. Outside of Greece, they have the best Greek food in the city."

"Okay, sounds good. What time?"

"I was hoping we could have dinner about 6 p.m., and then maybe do a club or something afterward."

"6:00 is fine, and we'll see about the afterward once we cross that bridge. So, I'll meet you there."

"Oh, I thought I was picking you up since it is a date."

"No, I'll drive my own car. Never know how the night will end."

"I'm hoping good, better than good."

"We'll see. So, I'll see you at 6. Talk to you later."

Nala hung up the phone before he could say goodbye. She was familiar with the restaurant. She and Kendrick had been there several times and the food was good. She figured at least she would get a good meal out of the deal.

***

Nala pulled into her driveway and parked her car. She could see a package on her walkway in front of the door. She got out of the car, walked over to it, and picked it up. Her heart sank, and her stomach did a butterfly dance. The name on the return address was Robert Randstad. She expected to receive a package from him after his execution, but to finally hold it in her hands was eerie. Nala unlocked the front door and went inside her house. She threw her keys and pocketbook on the table, took her coat off, and sat it on the chair. The package felt heavy as she made her way to the den. She sat down on the red, suede love seat and took off her boots. Her heart was pounding as she crossed her legs and stared at the package. Part of her wanted to rip it open, and the other part wanted to sit and imagine its contents. Nala's chest heaved up and down, and her stomach was flipping more rapidly now. For a minute, she thought she was going to vomit. She took a deep breath and began to open the folder. Her hands trembled as she removed the contents.

There were pictures and a hand-written letter. Nala looked through the pictures and couldn't believe what she was looking at. Her mother was quite young, with Robert Randstad. There were pictures of her from birth until she graduated from grad school. Nala sat the pictures down and walked over to the wine rack. She picked up a bottle of red wine and opened it. Her hands were shaking as she poured a full glass and began to drink. She could feel some of it trickling down her chin. Nala wiped it with the back of her hand and refilled her glass. She walked back to the love seat with her bottle and glass and sat down. Nala was fixated on the pictures. She couldn't believe her mother knew Randstad. Nala started to feel a lump in her throat. She thought she knew what the letter entailed. However, she didn't want to speculate, so she took another gulp of her wine and began reading.

*My dear Daisy,*

*If you're reading this letter, then I have been executed and am free from this repulsive world. I'm sure your head is spinning with a lot of questions. If you're anything like me, and we both know you are, then I would be sitting in my comfortable, favorite chair with a bottle of red wine. So, without further ado, let me tell you who you are. You're my Daisy. Well, that's what I called you after I saw you that one time. I met your mother in the summer of 1978. We were both in Wildwood, New Jersey vacationing. I was in what I considered a lifeless marriage, but I loved my wife. I met your mother one night while I was walking the boardwalk. Since you know who I am, I can tell you that I was lurking. She seemed as if she was in distress as she sat sipping her drink. I was drawn to her instantly. So, I got up the nerve and walked over to her. She looked up at me and her eyes were full of pain. To be honest, she reminded me of how my father used to look after my whorish mother would return home from one of her sexual escapades. He would look so lost and defeated. Your mother looked that way, so I had to stop and comfort her. I thought she was going to blow me off, but she didn't. I guess she needed me as much as I needed her. We talked for hours. It was like we knew each other for years. The next day, we met up and spent the day together. We walked the boardwalk, the beach, ate ice cream and just talked. Just from that one day I felt connected to your mother. Without getting too personal, the night I spent with your mother was magical. It was more than sex, it was spiritual. We spent the next few days together and then it was over. She was gone and so was I. The next time I heard from her was when she told me you were born and I was the father. I was ecstatic, but I knew nothing could come of it. We met back in Wildwood when you were about a month old. Spending time with you was the best time of my life. I called you Daisy because, while your mother was walking you in the stroller, a woman stopped us and asked if she could see the baby. We obliged, and she went on and on about how beautiful you were. Then she said, you were like a daisy because you represented purity and innocence. To me, that was perfect because out of the chaotic, unhappy lives we were both living at the time, something as sweet as you came from it. So, from that moment you were my daisy, although I never saw you again in person until you became the famous criminal psychologist. Oh, I was so proud of you.*

*I followed your career from your first case until you profiled and interviewed me. If anyone was going to catch and stop me, I wanted it to be you. Well, here we are. Now you know. You know who you are and where you come from. Ridding the world of bad people is in your blood. Your mother did it and so did I. You were destined to become who you are. Don't think what you're doing happened by chance. It was just a matter of time. There would have been no way that you could have resisted the urge to kill. It's in your DNA.*

*Along with this letter and photos is a safe deposit key. The only way you can retrieve what's inside the box is you'll have to go to my lawyer and he will direct you from there. He has been instructed to honor my final wishes. When the shock settles, you can phone him for further instructions. I know this has been a lot to digest and you're probably wondering if you're dreaming. No, you're awake, but you know I am always there with you. When you think you see something out of the corner of your eye, or you hear unexplainable noises, it's me watching over you and protecting you. I will always be here. Though I could never tell you who I was, I'm telling you now. I love you Daisy. And don't be too hard on your mother. She was in a place where her hands were tied as well. We are connected. You, me and your mom are like a triangle pendant where we meet at each point. Embrace your feelings and your lineage. I love you. Until we meet again, in your dreams.*

*Robert (dad)*

Nala picked up the wine bottle and began to drink. She had swallowed too much too fast and began to choke. Nala started coughing frantically as she hit her chest. Within minutes, she had gained control and was no longer choking. There was an array of emotions she felt as she sat the letter down next to her. One of the biggest emotions she felt was anger, but it was focused more on him. He was a big hypocrite. She felt like one too because she stood in front of her students and told them he killed those women because they didn't respect their marriage vows. Well, neither did he.

Nala knew he was a murderer, so she shouldn't expect him to have any integrity. On the other hand, there was her mother. Nala was angry at her, as well. She felt as if there was no truth in who she believed her parents to be. Nala could deal with having her aunt and uncle raise her as their own because her biological mother was in prison. But to have a father who is a notorious serial killer. She wondered if they knew. If they did, what were they thinking when she profiled him and contributed to him being sent to death row? As she thought about her parents knowing, it made her even angrier. Did anyone tell the truth in her family? Nala looked at the clock hanging on the wall and realized she should start getting ready for her "date." As pissed as she was, she needed someone to take it out on, and Bryce was the perfect person.

***

Nala made sure to park in a parking garage so she could change into her disguise. There was a parking garage about a block from the restaurant, which was perfect. She pulled into a parking spot and began the transformation. This time, she added false eyelashes because she liked how they looked on her. When she was done, she put her knife and ice pick in her oversized black Coach bag and headed out. Upon arriving at the restaurant, she glanced inside to see if Bryce had arrived, and he hadn't. As she was looking, he walked past her and entered the restaurant. He looked around for her, as well. That made Nala happy because he hadn't recognized her. She went inside, walked over to him, and tapped him on his shoulder.

"Yes," he said with a smile.

"It's me, Dominique."

"Huh, what?" he said, backing up and looking her over. "You changed."

"Is there a problem?"

"Oh, heck no. I like this version better. However, if I knew we were role-playing, I would have come as someone else too."

"And who would you like to have become?"

"Whoever you wanted me to be."

Nala smiled as he gawked her over like a flying vulture. She couldn't wait to get him alone. The hostess walked over to them and escorted them to their table. He portrayed himself as the perfect gentleman by pulling out her chair for her. She knew it was all a part of his act and what he hoped to get once the date was over. She knew the game, and she knew how to play it well.

"Hi, I'm Judy. I'll be your waitress for this evening. Can I start you with something to drink?"

"Yes, could you bring us a bottle of your red Merlot wine?"

"Sure. And here are the menus. I shall return."

They both thanked the waitress and began looking through the menu. Nala was familiar with the food and had already decided what she wanted, but she didn't want to let on that she had been there. As she perused the menu, she could feel Bryce glancing at her. To Nala, he seemed like a dog in heat, panting with his tongue hanging out of his mouth, dripping saliva. She thought about his wife and wondered what lie he told her about where he was going. Whatever the lie, his wife wouldn't have to worry about him anymore after tonight. Yeah, it would hurt for a while, but she would get over it with time, just like the other women. The waitress returned to the table and opened the wine. She poured each of them a glass with a smile.

"Are you ready to order?

"Yes. I will have the Cheese Saganaki with a side of grilled asparagus," said Nala.

"And you, sir?" the waitress asked, turning to Bryce.

"I'll have the Octopodi with the grilled vegetables," he replied.

"Okay. Your dinner will be here shortly. In the meantime, enjoy the wine."

The waitress walked away as they both picked up their glass and drank some. It tasted so good to Nala that she knew she could drink the entire bottle by herself. After the package she received earlier that day, all she really wanted to do was kill Bryce, put her feet up and drink the rest of the evening. But first things first.

"So, we finally made it happen. I'm glad we were able to hook up."

"Yeah, well, I'm sure it was hard getting out tonight for you. *Right*?"

"Absolutely not. Not trying to sound cocky or like I'm the shit, excuse my language, but my wife is pretty gullible. Anything I tell her she pretty much goes for."

"Really? Well, that's not nice. She seemed like a wonderful person when I saw her at the restaurant. Why are you looking to hurt her?"

"I'm not hurting her. She has no clue that I'm out with another woman. I wouldn't let on to that because I don't want to hurt her."

"Let me tell you something, Bryce, women know. You can act as if you're as careful as a lion walking across eggs, but something always tells. You may be acting nicer than usual, different cologne, smiling more, something. We may not catch it at first, but eventually we do."

"Listen, like I told you on the phone earlier, things are complicated. Marriage was never supposed to be in the equation."

"So, why did you marry her?"

"Okay, okay. I get the whole 'women banning together thing,' but I don't want to talk about my wife. I have a beautiful, sexy, intelligent woman sitting across from me who I am dying to get to know. Can we please change the subject? Let's enjoy this wonderful food that's coming soon, the wine and the ambiance. Okay?"

"Cool."

The waitress had come with their food, and Nala was surprised to see Bryce lower his head to pray. After all, the devil was an Angel first, so nothing should surprise her. Nala had forgotten how good the food was there. She hadn't been there in quite some time—the last time being with Kendrick to celebrate a promotion. Nala started to feel a little nostalgic, and it surprised her. When it came to Kendrick, any thoughts of happiness were null and void. He had lost those privileges the moment he cheated on her for the last time. As she sat there eating, looking at the snake across from her, she wondered what Kendrick's line was to the few women he cheated with. Did he say, "he was unhappy at home" or "it's complicated" or better yet, "we've outgrown one another?" If he did use any of those lines, they were farthest from the truth in Nala's book. She believed they were happy. If she had to bet her life on it, she would undeniably say they were happy. At this point, it didn't matter. They were history, and Nala was a killer.

Bryce finished up his meal as Nala's was slowly coming to an end. He poured them another glass of wine and began to drink it. All he could think about was how he was going to get Nala in bed. Just thinking about her thick legs over his shoulders and him pouncing inside of her made him horny as hell. Sex with his wife was okay, but he had a feeling sex with Nala would be unlike anything he'd ever experienced. He felt Nala was a freak. She presented herself as classy and reserved, but, in Bryce's experience, those are the ones who turned it out in the bedroom.

"So, what's up for us after dinner? Are you the club type?"

"No. I haven't been the club type since college. They're all the same, and after a while, it gets old. I could think of better ways to spend my time."

"Oh really? How?"

"Watching a good black and white suspense movie, reading, or just listening to some music while sipping some red wine."

"Well, we can do that. I personally like listening to some music and sipping some red wine."

"Oh, do you now? And where are we supposed to do this?"

"The weather isn't bad. We can take a drive to Fairmount Park, park by Boathouse Row and just relax. I can order a bottle of wine to go, and my car is filled with CDs from Al Jarreau to Mary J. Blige. So, you want to go?"

Nala looked outside, and the sun was beginning to set. If she was still going to go through with her plans, she needed more of a secluded place. Boathouse Row was an active area of the park, and she would run the risk of being seen. She knew whatever she suggested to Bryce he would be game for. There was a nice part of the park behind the art museum she discovered some years back. That could be the place. It was a cold chill in the air, so there would probably not be many, if any, people walking about.

"I have another idea. You can follow me in my car. I know just the spot."

"Cool. So, are we done? Do you want any dessert?"

"No, I'm stuffed. We can just go."

Bryce gestured for the waitress so he could pay the bill. As Nala gathered her belongings, she looked at the entrance to the restaurant and saw Jessica walk in. Of all the restaurants in Philly, her student had to choose the same one as her. Nala's heart began to beat fast, and she knew she had to remain calm to not bring any attention to herself. Bryce paid the bill and left a tip. He helped her with her coat as she tried not to look the way of Jessica.

"Are you ready beautiful?" asked Bryce.

"Mmmm, hmmm," she said, walking quickly to the door.

As she reached the door, she and Jessica glanced at one another. Jessica dropped her car keys as she fumbled to open her pocketbook to put them in. Bryce, nearly bumping into her, reached down to pick them up as he followed behind Nala.

"Thank you," Jessica said, looking him in the eyes with a smile and taking her keys from his hand.

"No problem," he responded, rushing behind to catch up to Nala.

Nala couldn't tell if Jessica noticed her, and it made her feel extremely uncomfortable. Bryce followed Nala outside as she hurriedly walked down the street. She wanted to get as far away from the restaurant as she could.

"Yo, slow down. Where's the fire?"

"I was starting to feel a little overheated. I'm okay now."

"Okay. Well, I'm parked around the corner. Where are you parked?"

"How about I just go and get my car and meet you back here. Okay?"

Nala turned away and headed for the parking garage. She was still a little on edge about seeing Jessica, but time would tell if she noticed who she was. Nala felt confident she was not recognizable when she put on her disguise, but you never know. She began to wrestle with the idea if killing Bryce tonight was smart. Was it an omen running into Jessica? Her gut was saying go home, but her desire to kill was saying go for it.

When she reached the parking lot and got in her car, she sat for a while, contemplating what to do. She had waited for this night to do away with Bryce since she met him. But now she wasn't sure. Nala took the knife out of her pocketbook and ran her finger across the sharp-edged blade. Feeling the sharpness of it gave her a rush. She hadn't felt that way in a while, and she missed it. Nala looked at herself in the rearview mirror and mouthed, "you got this." She started the car and drove down the three levels, so she could pay the bill. She inserted the money into the slot and drove off once the gate was lifted. On her way back to the restaurant, her phone rang, and it was Bryce. She looked at it and chuckled. While approaching the restaurant, she could see a car double-parked in front of it. She rode past it, looked inside, and honked as she kept driving. Bryce sped off behind her, and they started on their drive.

Bryce continued to call her phone, but she wouldn't answer. She just laughed as she drove to Fairmount Park and to the area where she would do her do. Nala pulled up under some trees to park, and Bryce followed her. It was very secluded, and that's what she needed. She sat for a second and then opened her car door. Nala could feel the knife inside her coat pocket as she walked to his car. Bryce looked confused as she got in the backseat behind him. He was about to join her, but she shook her head no.

"Lay back, baby. There's no rush. We got all the time in the world."

"Man, I like you. First the disguise, now a game. Shit girl, you're turning me on."

"Am I? So, where did you tell your wife you were going tonight?"

"Why is that so important to you? Whatever I told her, it worked because I'm here. So, let's make the most of it. Okay?"

"Okay. Your problem, not mine. Just relax then," she said, leaning his head back on the headrest.

Nala began rubbing his neck as her hand slid down his shirt to rub his chest. Bryce smiled as he began to enjoy the massage. "You like that?" she asked while placing a kiss on his neck.

"Hell yeah, girl. I'm getting hard as fuck. Let me come back there with you?" he anxiously said.

"If I let you come back here, then you have to tell me what you told your wife to get out of the house."

"Damn girl, okay, okay. I said I was meeting with my frat brother for drinks."

"And she said?"

"What? She said, 'okay, cool. Have a good time.' Now, can I come back there with you?"

"Not yet. So, she was fine with you going out? Whatever makes her husband happy, it's okay with her. Right?"

"Yeah, I guess."

Nala reached her hand in her pocket and pulled out the knife. She continued to kiss his neck as she got a firm grip on the blade. Bryce began to mumble things he wanted to do to her, but it sickened her to her stomach. All she could do was imagine his wife being home, watching TV or reading and waiting for him to return. In her mind, her husband was out having a good time with his frat brothers. Unbeknownst to her, he was trying to fuck another woman and act as if it's justified. It sent shockwaves through her body, and she was ready to deal with him.

"You know what, Bryce?"

"What baby?"

"You make me sick," she said, plunging the knife into his neck.

Bryce gasped as he reached up and held where she stabbed. The blood gushed from his neck and seeped through his fingers. He tried to speak, but there was a gurgling sound coming from his mouth. Nala plunged the knife back into his neck, and Bryce's body stopped moving. She wiped the blade off on his shirt and opened the car door using her coat, just the way she entered. Nala looked at him and thought to herself that he never looked better.

## Chapter 10

There had been several news stories of Nala's latest victim's body being found in the park since yesterday. The news reports were all the same, but they didn't start out that way. At first, he was an unidentified African American male, but today, a name was put on the body. The name was Bryce Wilkins. Nala loved seeing the aftermath of her work. Yellow tape, news reporters and police searching for clues always gave her a rush. She knew, once the body was found two days ago, Detective Chase would be calling her. After all, she had just reported she didn't know when or if the killer would strike again. Then low and behold, she does that evening—what a coincidence.

Nala sat at the airport, sipping on a hot cup of coffee, waiting for her plane to board. She was on her way to get her mother. So much had happened in the week it felt like it happened over a span of a month. She found out early in the week that Robert Randstad was her father, and on Wednesday, she snuffed the life out of a sorry ass excuse for a man. Nala couldn't wait to confront her mother about Robert. She couldn't believe she didn't tell her when they began to bond. As far as the murder she just committed, she would feel her mother out first before she decided to tell her or not. Nala was finishing up her coffee when they began to call for first class. She picked up her brown, leather briefcase and pocketbook and walked to the stewardess, handing her a boarding pass. The woman politely looked at it, smiled and gestured for Nala to get on the plane.

***

When Nala landed in L.A., the sun was shining, and the air was thick. She was ready to pick up her mother and get back to her home, so they could begin a real relationship. Before getting her mother, she wanted to kick up her feet and have a glass of wine. When she reached the hotel, she went to the lounge and sat at the bar. A few people were sitting and enjoying the coolness the hotel had to offer. As Nala sat thinking about how she would approach her mother, the bartender took her order of red wine. Nala smiled and thanked him as he sat it in front of her. She picked it up and sipped, trying not to drink it all in one swallow. It tasted like heaven to her as she couldn't help herself and drank it all. She gestured for the bartender and held up her finger, representing one more.

"Thirsty, huh?" he asked, pouring another glass of wine.

"Thirsty, tired. Long flight, and this is relaxing."

"Where are you from?"

"Philly."

"Ohhh, the city of brotherly love."

"And sisterly affection," she said, sipping the wine with a smile.

"Well, from what we hear, one of the sistas isn't too fond of the brothas over there. You guys have a serial killer on your hands, huh?"

"Yeah, that's what they say."

"Because that's what it is," he said, chuckling. "What's wrong? The men aren't treating you ladies right?"

"It's not all men. Just men who cheat on their wives, from what I understand."

"Wow. Hey, look, I get it that cheating is wrong, but murder is just as wrong. If this woman is going to go around killing all the cheating married men, she'd be killing forever. Unfortunately, that's a way of life for some men."

"And evidently, killing them is a way of life for her. Thanks." She got up and left a hefty tip for the bartender. Nala headed to the elevator feeling pretty good and went to her room.

***

There were an array of emotions going through Nala as she walked into the facility to pick up her mother. The place reminded her of a college dormitory at the end of the semester. There were a lot of people moving about as they picked up their loved ones. Once the head of the institution was indicted, people began to remove their family members. Although they were assured the incidents that occurred would never happen again, the place was tainted. Nala panned the room and saw her mother sitting on a couch looking around. She was dressed as if she was about to consult a potential client. Nala knew her mother wasn't crazy for what she had done. She just couldn't control the thing inside of her that was dying to come out. Nala knew that feeling all too well.  The urge to kill felt like contractions and the only relief was to release what caused the pain. That's how Nala felt each time she got the urge. She wanted to believe it was the same for her mother.

Nala locked eyes with her mother as she walked towards her. She stood up, and the two hugged tightly. Her mother reached down and picked up her Louis Vuitton clutch purse. Nala had already arranged for her belongings to be shipped to her home. She had asked Pam to be there when the delivery arrived and she agreed. Her mother only had an overnight bag, which Nala grabbed, and the two walked out to the waiting cab.

The ride to the hotel was somewhat silent except for a few "you look good" and "glad to see you" comments in between. Nala would save the big finale once they arrived at the hotel. The two just held hands and looked out the window. Nala could sense her mother soaking up the air, the ride, the freedom. She hadn't been able to go out on her own for the last thirty years. Nala couldn't begin to imagine what she was feeling. She hoped it was nothing but pure enjoyment and relief.

It felt good to be able to have her mother back after all the years she was gone. Nala didn't want their reunion to be clouded by the murders Nala was committing. She wanted her mother to be free from that memory, but Nala felt like she was just getting started. It felt good to her, and she didn't know if she could stop. She didn't know if she wanted to.

## Chapter 11

While in L.A., Nala decided she would wait until they returned home before she sprang the news about Robert Randstad on her mother. She wanted her first night as a free woman to be nothing but peaceful and relaxing. Letting on that she knew Robert was her father might have sent her mother to another place mentally where she didn't need to go. When they arrived home, her mother's luggage was in the room Nala had specified to Pam where she wanted it. Dominique walked around Nala's home with a smile. She was extremely proud of everything she had accomplished. Nala truly reminded her of her younger self.

"You have such a beautiful home, baby."

"Thanks, Mom. Come on, let's go sit down in the living room. Are you hungry, thirsty?"

"No, I'm fine. If anything, I'm just a little tired from the flight, but I'm glad it's over, and I'm finally home."

"Do you want to take a nap? Your room is ready for you. We just have to unpack."

"I'm fine, Nala. Calm down. You've done so much for me already. I'm not a sick, old, feeble woman who can't do for herself. Anything I need, I'll get it. Okay?" She smiled.

"Okay. I just want you to be fine."

"And I am. But I can tell since yesterday something is on your mind. What is it?"

Nala thought it was so uncanny how her mother could read her. Although she wanted to address the issue about Randstad, she just wanted to enjoy the peaceful moment. Later in the day, she would call her mother and father to talk

107

to them. Nala had planned to have a little welcome home dinner party later in the week, but she wanted her to get accustomed to being free for now.

Dominique sat waiting for Nala to tell her what was on her mind. She secretly hoped Nala would tell her she killed that lying ex-husband of hers and his whore, but she didn't want to put any ideas in the air. Dominique believed there were things worse than death, and if Nala played her cards right, she could inflict that upon them both.

"So, what's going on?"

Nala got up and walked over to the table and opened the drawer. She pulled out the folder she had received from Randstad and handed it to her mother. Dominique smiled as she pulled out the contents of the envelope. She unfolded the letter and began reading. Nala slowly sat down, watching her mother. Her face was glowing as Nala watched her eyes move back and forth from reading. Dominique chuckled at a moment as if a memory had taken hold of her. After she finished the letter, she gently folded it back and put it away.

"I'll have that drink now. And make it wine," she said, sitting back in her chair as if lost in a nostalgic moment.

Nala stood up and walked over to the minibar. She poured two glasses of red wine and handed one to her mother. Dominique took a sip and let out a sigh. Nala drank most of the wine in her glass in one gulp while waiting to hear what her mother had to say. She was anxious, and her sweaty palms and rapid heartbeat confirmed it.

"The Robert the world knew, the one you interviewed and thought was a monster wasn't the one I knew. The four days I spent with him were some of the best days of my life. He was nothing like the man who I had to share with the world. I didn't know Robert, the serial killer. I didn't know Robert, the man who brutally killed seven women and did horrific things to them. The Robert I knew was gentle and calm."

"So, did Mom and Dad know who my father was? Did Daddy even know?"

"No. I never told anyone. Your Daddy raised you believing you were his daughter, and he truly loved you. If there was ever a time I wanted to tell the truth, I could never, especially after everyone saw Robert as a horrific serial killer."

"I don't know how to feel about this. I'm just learning about you and gaining a relationship. Now I must deal with one of the most notorious serial killers in the world being my father. How does a person grasp that their parent is a murderer? The Robert you knew and seemed to have loved wasn't the Robert I knew. He was a vicious sociopath who murdered seven women and cut out their eyes. How do I deal with someone like that being my father?"

"Actually, you don't have to. He's dead. You had no relationship with him, so it's as if you never knew him."

"Really? So, you're saying because I didn't know he was my father anyway I should just disregard the fact that I know now? How am I supposed to do that?

"Keep living like you were before."

"There were pictures of me, twenty to be exact. Why?"

"By the time I learned of who the world knew Robert to be, I had already sent him pictures of you each year. Although I was hurt, I was more so confused. I tried to separate that man from the one I knew. So, I continued to send him a picture of you each year. He could see you grow and change. It was as if he was a part of your life when he wasn't."

"But how were you able to send him pictures of me if you were in the facility?"

"I always told your mother to send me a duplicate picture, so I could have one and send him the other. She didn't know why I asked for duplicate pictures, but she sent them at my request."

Nala filled her glass of wine to the brim and drank it down. She thought talking about the Randstad situation with Dominique would be easy, but it was anything but easy. There was an array of emotions she felt. Some of it was anger. She didn't know if she was angrier at her mother for never telling her the truth or for having a murderer for a father. But how could her mother tell her the truth? It would have been far more complicated with her father believing he was her dad. Also, how do you tell a child their father is a serial killer? Nala assumed it had to be just as bad for her mother.

She thought about Randstad's wishes of not being hard on her mother, sat next to Dominique, and looked at her. Her eyes welled with tears as Dominique took her hand and held it in hers. She knew her daughter was in pain, confused, angry and even hurt. Dominique felt Nala must've felt betrayed on so many levels. She believed the parents who raised her were her biological parents for all her life, but she found out they weren't. Then to have a blow like learning an infamous serial killer is your father is enough to push anyone off a ledge. Dominique understood the betrayal and pain, but she hated her daughter had to feel it.

"There was also a key with instructions to contact his lawyer. What do you think it is?

"Knowing Robert, something that will set you up for life."

"I'm good financially if it's money. I don't want it."

Dominique smiled and patted Nala's hand. She was definitely their child, stubborn and too proud. Dominique felt Nala needed time to digest everything she had just learned. It was a lot within the week, so Dominique decided not to pry or force her to do anything she didn't want to do. When Nala was ready, she would go to her, and Dominique knew it would be sooner than later.

"So, let's change the subject. What have you been up to lately? Have you been naughty or nice? Have you been taming the beast?" Dominique asked with a cunning grin.

"Uh, where did that question come from?"

"From a mother knowing her daughter. If I turn on the news, I won't see any news reports of any unsolved murders of married men, will I?"

"Um, I don't know. You might?"

Nala laughed as she felt the pit of her stomach drop. She wasn't going to tell her what she had done to good ole' Bryce. She would let her find out about his demise from the news and put two and two together. Even though she came from the DNA of two killers, Nala didn't want to flaunt what she did. After all, it was still murder, although it felt sweet.

\*\*\*

Dominique had fallen asleep after dinner and hadn't had a chance to talk to her sister. Nala figured she would call her tomorrow and invite them over for a few days to catch up. She was sure her mother wanted to see her sister. It had been many years for her, as well. It was close to the evening news airing, so Nala poured herself a glass of wine and sat on the sofa. She crossed her legs and turned on the TV. Nothing sparked her interest, and there was nothing pertaining to Bryce's murder. As the news was about to end, there was a recap of the week's top stories. Nala perked up and continued drinking.

*"Police are still searching for leads in the murder of Bryce Wilkins. Wilkins's body was found on Wednesday in a section of Fairmount Park in Philadelphia. He was found with multiple stab wounds to the neck and upper body. Police believe he is the latest victim of the serial killer who police have dubbed as "Lady Ice." A $50,000 reward has been offered for the capture and conviction of the perpetrator. Wilkins is survived by his wife and two children."*

Nala felt a quick sign of remorse for his wife and children, but the feeling had gone as quickly as it came. She felt they were better off without him. Nala filled her glass with more wine and leaned back. She was starting to feel a buzz as the wine began to calm her from head to toe. Within seconds, she was asleep.

It was almost 2 a.m. when Nala opened her eyes to Dominique standing over her. She could feel someone had been watching her, and it made her feel uneasy. Nala sat up and looked at her mother, who seemed to be in a trance. Dominique's eyes were focused on Nala, but it was as if she was staring right through her.

"Mom," Nala said, standing up slowly. "Mom, are you alright?"

Dominique was silent, and it began to scare Nala. She didn't know what was wrong, and she was afraid to touch her. If her mother was sleepwalking, Nala had heard people sleepwalking shouldn't be touched. However, she had to do something. Nala slowly touched her mother's hand and called her name. Without incident, her mother's eyes blinked, and she looked at Nala with a smile.

"Hey, what are you still doing up? You can't sleep?" Dominique asked.

"Uh, sit down, Mom," Nala said, helping her to sit. "Are you alright?"

"Why you ask?" she said curiously.

"Well, because I woke up and you were just standing there staring at me. I called your name and you didn't budge. Do you sleepwalk, Mom?"

A looked appeared on Dominique's face that Nala was trying to interpret. It was a look between "I'm caught" and "I'm ashamed." Whatever Dominique thought she couldn't share with Nala, she had to. Dominique let out a sigh and gave Nala a smile. "How about you make your mother some nice, hot tea?" she asked, getting up and heading towards the kitchen.

Nala followed behind her, hoping she was going to open up about what just happened. Dominique took two mugs from the cupboard and sat down. After Nala put the water in the teapot, she sat at the breakfast table across from her mother. Although Nala had to be at work in a few hours, it seemed. She needed to hear what her mother had to say. Dominique's eyes looked sad. Nala could feel whatever she needed to tell her was hard.

"Well, um," she said, clearing her throat. "I hope I didn't scare you too much," she said with a nervous chuckle.

"No, you didn't scare me, but I was concerned."

"Good, I'm glad. You know, part of the reason I was released was because of my involvement in getting that bitch arrested for what she was doing to us."

"Yes, I know."

"Well, those nights we had to be with men were degrading. She tried to make us believe we were the cream of the crop and we should be appreciative we were chosen, but that was far from the truth. Each time some strange man touched me, fondled me, kissed me, I was sick, just sick! I knew I couldn't go anywhere physically when their rich, manicured hands ran across my breast and my body, but I could leave mentally, and I did."

"So, you basically zoned out."

"Yeah. I taught myself how to do it, and eventually, I was a master at it. However, physically leaving your body that way transcends you into another realm, like your dreams."

Nala looked at her with a perplexed look on her face. She felt like she understood what Dominique was talking about, but she wasn't sure. Nala was taken back to the experience she had with the banging on her door. It wasn't until Randstad had been executed that the banging stopped. She couldn't explain it, but it seemed more than a coincidence. However, she wanted to hear more about what Dominique had to say. Nala wanted a glass of wine instead of the tea, but she would be getting ready for work soon. Drinking wine would put her in an entirely different place, which she couldn't go at the time. So, she added her two sugars and cream and took a sip of her tea.

"What do you mean?"

"This may sound weird to you, but sometimes I don't think my dreams are dreams. Sometimes, I feel like I'm living what is going on, but my body is still here, just a shell."

"Hmmm. Really? In what way?"

"Okay, well, you said I was standing over you zoned out. Right?"

"Yeah, Mmm-hmm."

"So, I don't remember that. I don't remember getting out of bed, walking downstairs and coming in watching over you."

"So, what do you remember?"

"Dreaming about Robert and him telling me how happy he was that we were together."

"Interesting."

"Not really. He always comes to me in my dreams. Without freaking you out too much, I'm sure it was him who made me come down here to check on you. Only I have no recollection of it. I remember my dream in the spiritual sense, not the physical sense."

"Wait, huh?" Nala said, thinking more about getting a glass of wine.

"The spirit of me was with Robert in my dream, and we were talking about you. The physical part of me, meaning the shell of me, the body, if you will, was left in the bed. That was what you saw standing over you. I didn't awake until the spirit part of me returned to the shell of me. Do you understand what I'm saying?"

"I think so."

"When I was in the facility and had to be with those men, I left and went on a whole different plato. They never fully had me. "

Nala sat trying not to look at her mother like she was crazy because she actually believed her. Dominique had just given her proof the banging she was experiencing was indeed from Randstad. In hindsight, Nala felt like it was him telling her that although she couldn't see him, he would always be there. Nala still had mixed feelings about that. She didn't want him to always be there. She didn't need his protection, and she definitely didn't want to be linked to him as his daughter. He was still, in her eyes, a sadistic murderer.

Nala knew both of her parents were killers, but she felt she and her mother killed out of necessity. Randstad, on the other hand, was just a twisted sociopath in her opinion. Nala could sense the connection Dominique had with Randstad, and she didn't want to diminish that. However, she couldn't understand how Dominique could have loved him and knew what he was doing. Maybe because her recollection of him is viewing pictures of seven women brutally murdered and having him tell her it was God's will. To Nala, that was sick.

They both sat drinking their coffee in silence for a few minutes. The time was moving along. Soon, the sun would be peeping in her kitchen window. Nala had a class to meet with the students working on their respected cases. She was interested in hearing what they came up with. She also figured she would give Detective Chase a call. Something in her gut told her she needed to watch him. It was nothing he said per se, but it was just a feeling she had. Nala finished her coffee and looked at the clock on the wall that read 4:20 am. She figured she could close her eyes for at least an hour or so before getting ready for work.

"Well, I'm going to go and try and relax before I have to get up. Are you okay?"

"Yes, and I'm sorry I disturbed your sleep. Go and get some rest."

"No problem," Nala said, getting up from the kitchen table.

"Uh Nala, have you heard from your ex and his girlfriend lately?"

"Actually, not since they sicked the cops on me. Why you ask?"

"I don't want you to forget about them. Comfortability should be the last thing they have. Don't let them forget how they disrupted and changed your life. You hear me?"

"Yeah, Mom, I do."

"Okay, go and get some sleep. I'll take care of these few dishes."

Thanks. And I'm going to leave Mom's number, so you two can talk. I'm hoping they can come this week for a few days."

"Yes, sure. We'll talk, now go and get some rest."

Nala went into her bedroom and poured a glass of wine that was on her nightstand. After the early morning with Dominique, she needed something stronger than coffee. She took a few sips then gulped the rest down. Afterward, she filled her glass several more times until the bottle was empty. Nala was sure that would give her two good hours of sleep. She sat on her bed and fell backward with her arms sprawled out, staring at the ceiling. Her body felt relaxed as her eyes blinked slowly. It didn't take long before they closed and she was asleep.

## Chapter 12

It was a struggle for Nala to get up. It seemed as if she had just lied down to fall asleep when the alarm clock buzzed loudly. She rolled over and put the pillow over her head. It felt like she had only closed her eyes a few minutes ago, but the alarm clock read an hour had gone by. Nala sat up and looked around the room before getting up and walking into the bathroom. She turned on the water in the shower and took off her nightshirt and panties. Teasing the water with her foot to make sure it wasn't too hot, she stepped in and let the water run down her body. Nala washed and got out, knowing she was pressed for time. After she dressed, she peeked into her mother's bedroom to check on her. Surprisingly, she was not in bed. Nala went downstairs and looked around but didn't see her anywhere.

"Mom," she called out, checking the movie room, her den and the family room. She had already checked the living room and kitchen. As she began to panic, she saw the front door slowly open and her mother walking in. "Mom," Nala said, quickly walking over to her and giving her a hug.

"What's wrong?" her mother asked.

"You scared me to death. I looked everywhere for you and couldn't find you. Please don't do that again."

"Do what?"

"Leave without telling me."

"I didn't. I came into your room, woke you up and got the code to the alarm system. I told you I was going for a walk to get in my exercise and you said okay."

"You did. When?"

"Maybe about an hour ago. You were really tired, and I hated waking you, but I didn't want to open the front door and have the police here because of the alarm system going off."

"Oh wow, I don't remember that. Well, I'm glad you're okay. Listen, I won't be gone too long. Will you be okay?"

"Yes, I'll be okay. I have everything I need. You go to work now, and I'll see you when you get home."

"If you want, I can work from home."

"Nala, go to work. I'm good. I may do some reading from all those books you have in there."

"Oh wait, I'll give you Mom's number. You can call her."

Nala got a piece of paper and a pen from the table in the foyer and wrote down the phone number. Dominique took it with a smile and put it in her pocket. Nala put on her jacket and picked up her pocketbook and briefcase. She hesitantly walked to the front door. She turned around and looked at Dominique, hoping she would need her to stay.

"Are you...."

"Nala, have a good day. I'll be fine. Now go," she said, giving her a soft shove out the door.

*** 

On the way to work, Nala thought a lot about what Dominique said regarding Kendrick and Crystal. It had been too quiet, and she wondered what that meant. Crystal should be moving quite along in her pregnancy and, knowing her for the little conniving bitch she was, it wouldn't be long before she made her way into Nala's presence to show off her belly bump. So, before she could get Nala, Nala would get her. She looked at the time on the dashboard and saw she had more time than she thought before her class was to begin. She attributed it to her putting her foot to the pedal while driving the highway.

When Nala reached work, she drove on the side of campus where Kendrick worked. She had no clue what she was going to say if she ran into him. The divorce proceeding was still in process, and he had signed the paper. So, there was no reason for her to be on that side of campus. Nala pulled in a parking space and sat. She tapped her hand on the steering wheel and tried to figure something out. After all, she did have colleagues who she conversed with on that side of campus, so she could just inadvertently visit one of them. But how would that look? At that moment, she didn't care. She fixed her hair and retouched her lipstick before getting out of the car. She entered the building, a few people spoke to her, and she stopped for small talk. During her conversation, Nala felt Kendrick's presence walking behind her. The sounds his stride made as his feet touched the floor and the smell that immediately filled the hallway was that of her soon-to-be ex-husband. Nala didn't turn around. She knew Kendrick noticed her. How could he not? The form-fitting lavender dress that hugged her curves and the firmness and thickness of her calves on her pretty chocolate legs was all he needed to not turn away. Nala giggled at the small talk she was having, but her attention was elsewhere. She could feel him getting closer, and within seconds Kendrick was standing next to her.

"Good morning, ladies, "he said.

"Good morning. Dr. Jordan, it was good talking to you. Don't be a stranger."

"I won't, Professor Harvey. Take care."

She walked away, leaving Kendrick and Nala to whatever was going to come. Professor Harvey was aware of the love triangle between the Jordans and Crystal, and she was not pleased with it. Secretly, she despised Kendrick and Crystal, but she had to remain professional and unbiased. Nala felt as if she could hear Kendrick's heart beating rapidly. She knew he was nervous. Everyone knew who was to blame for their breakup, and she was sure he had his fair share of gossip and pointing fingers. It was moments like this one that gave her extreme joy. She found satisfaction in watching Kendrick's nervous gestures and smile.

"So, how have you been?" he asked.

"Good."

"You rarely get to this side of campus anymore. What brings you to my house?" he asked with a grin.

"Business."

"Oh, business? Are you sure?"

Nala chuckled at the sudden arrogance he portrayed. He was just like every other man. They think the world and everyone in it owes them something. It doesn't matter if they hurt someone or break vows that were promised to be kept; in their mind, at the end of the day, they're still wanted. Unfortunately, that was far from the truth. She didn't want him. She loathed him. She despised him. She hated him. Her heart was once his, and he broke it not one, not two, but three times. Even after all the "I'm sorry," "I love you," I want no one else," he still fuckin cheated and broke her heart. So, in front of her stood the enemy, and it was only a matter of time before he was annihilated.

"Am I sure? I know you don't think you had anything to do with my visit. You lost those privileges a long time ago. Please, don't flatter yourself. There's nothing about you and me that says us."

"It was just a question. Listen Nala, I......"

"Oh, bitch alert. Here comes your *lady*."

Kendrick turned around and saw Crystal walking toward them. Her expression said it all. Kendrick wasn't in the mood to explain why he talked to his wife and why he hadn't told her goodbye before leaving this morning. He wasn't in the mood to see her at all. But he knew he'd better act like it if he was to get any peace at home. Crystal felt her stomach doing flips as she got closer to them. She feared Nala, and Nala knew it. Dominique was right in saying that once you incite fear in someone, you're in control of their life. Crystal reached Kendrick, took him by the arm, and yanked it, trying to turn him to face her. He looked at her, trying not to show how he felt, which was annoyed.

"Hey, what's up?" Kendrick asked.

"Uh, you tell me," she said with an attitude.

"Don't worry, sweetie. He's yours. I'm done with him."

"Excuse me, Nala, but I was talking to Kendrick, if you don't mind," Crystal said with authority.

"Crystal, it's not like that. Chill," Kendrick said.

"Like what, Kendrick? Last time I checked, we were still colleagues and even more than that married. If I want to talk to my *husband,* I can. What you need to do is wait until we're done and stand over there like the little puppet you are and shut the fuck up."

"Wha, what? Kendrick! Are you going to let her talk to me like that?"

"Girl, please, what do you expect him to do? Defend your honor? Don't you know there's no true loyalty to a hoe? Damn, you stupid."

"Alright, Nala, chill," Kendrick said.

"You got it," she said, laughing. "Oh, and be careful. You're in your what, second trimester? Things can still happen," she said and walked away.

"Did you hear her, Kendrick? She's threatening me. I'll call Detective Jackson on you, Nala! You hear me!" she yelled to her as she walked away laughing.

*** 

When Nala made it to class, she felt like she owned the world. Most of her students were there when she walked into the classroom. She sat her briefcase and pocketbook on the podium since she didn't have time to take it to her office. The rest of the students entered the class as Nala took her cellphone out of her pocketbook. A text message had come through, and she was sure it was from Kendrick. She opened it and it read, "We need to talk. Hit me back or call me to let me know when and where. Please, it's important." She also saw she had three missed calls from her mother. She figured Dominique must've called and talked to her, but she wasn't sure. She would find out later when she phoned Dominique. Nala sat the phone on the desk and turned her attention to her students.

"Good morning. So, you've had some time to review your cases. I would like to hear from you all about what you've found, what you've learned and so forth. Okay, who's going first?"

"I will," Jessica blurted out. Nala got a sick feeling to the pit of her stomach. She hadn't seen Jessica since she ran into her at the restaurant. Nala was eager to find out if she learned anything.

"Okay, you're on," Nala said, walking in front of the podium and leaning against it.

"Okay, well, I went through the crime scenes photos and police reports and...."

"Sorry to interrupt, but before you begin, tell us which case you are working on."

"Oh yeah, I'm working on the murder case of the serial killer dubbed Lady Ice in Philly. So, as I said, I've been going over the crime scene pics and reading the police report. All I'm getting from the photos is an unsub who is methodical but extremely angry. But let me back up. This case has just gotten personal per se because I actually saw the latest victim of Lady Ice."

"Really!?" said one of the students.

"Yes. Okay, listen. Last week, I went to dinner at this Indian restaurant downtown in Philly. As I'm walking in, this woman brushes past me really quickly, and the guy following behind her bumps into me. I drop my keys, and he reaches down to pick them up. We were practically kissing when he handed them back to me. That's how close we were. I remember he was really cute, and his eyes were gorgeous. I said thank you, he said you're welcome, and he walked out."

"So, how do you know he was the same guy?"

"Well, because the other day I was watching the news, and the story of his murder came on. His name was Bryce Wilkins. When I saw his picture, I dropped my cup of coffee, and my mouth flew open. I immediately knew it was the same guy. I yelled to my boyfriend to come see the news. After it was over, I just sat down and tried to get myself together. I couldn't believe it. Here I run into a man who was murdered, and I'm working on the case of other murders committed by the same perp. I was floored."

"How are you so sure it's the same perp?" asked Nala.

"With the information given on the news and the information learned in the police reports, it's safe to say it's the same person."

"But what clues, better yet evidence, do you have to substantiate that? How do you know it's not a copycat?"

"Okay, I'm getting there. When the news has reported the murders, they never give a physical description of anyone seen with any victims. The report is always about them. As I'm reading each of the reports and statements taken from people at a few of the crime scenes, one thing has been common."

"And that is?" Nala asks with a dry throat and sweaty palms.

"A woman with long black hair and black shades."

"Hey, didn't you say a lady brushed past you as you were walking in?" asked the same student.

"I sure did. And guess what, she had long black hair and was wearing black shades. And to make it even better, she's the woman the guy was chasing behind. They were together."

"OMG, Jessica! You saw Lady Ice."

"I believe I did."

Nala stood trying to remain cool as a cucumber while the students began talking about the case and how Jessica could be the one to help solve it. This was the first time Nala felt a little nervous about being caught. As she stood watching the future criminal psychologist, she began to think it may not have been a good idea to have her case as one of the cases to work on. Nala's mind was a million miles away, but she had to regroup quickly. She was in control, and she wouldn't get caught unless she wanted to. The good thing in Nala's mind was that Jessica worshipped her. Nala knew Jessica would do practically anything she said and think anything she told her to. She was still in control and had been since the first time she killed. Nala walked behind the podium and tapped it with her pen loudly. Her students stopped talking and turned to her. She smiled and walked back in front of the podium with her arms crossed. Her students looked at her with wide eyes waiting for what she had to say. Nala looked at Jessica and smiled.

"So, Ms. Jessica, what is your next move?" asked Nala.

"Well, to be honest, I want to go to the police, but I didn't know if I should. That's why I waited for class today to see what you thought?"

"You're the investigator on this case. Remember class, this is your case. I'm only here to advise."

"Okay," Jessica said, writing down some notes in her notepad.

Nala began asking the other students about their cases and information that had been obtained. Jessica knew what she had to do. She reached in her pocketbook and pulled out her wallet. She took the business cards out and fumbled through them until she came across detective Chase's card. Jessica put it inside her notepad and turned her attention to the class.

After class was over, Nala asked to speak with Jessica. Although Nala told her students their case was theirs alone to solve, she wasn't stupid. She had to make sure she wasn't out of the loop in any way. Nala had to be privy to any and everything she knew. Jessica stood in front of the class as the other students left and waited to hear what Nala had to say.

"I didn't want to say this in front of the other students. If I did, I would be bombarded with requests to help. However, if there is anything you need me to do, just ask. But, it stays between us, okay?"

"Sure, Dr. Jordan, I appreciate that."

"So, have you decided what you're going to do with the information you have?"

"Yes, I'm going to call Detective Chase and ask if I could come to see him."

"Just so happens, I'm going to see him today. Would you like to ride with me?"

"Yeah, sure. I appreciate that."

"Okay, let's say in about an hour? Are you free?"

"Yes, I am. I'll meet you at your office."

"Sounds good."

Jessica and Nala walked out of the classroom with Nala going to her office and Jessica headed in the other direction. When Nala got to her office, she couldn't believe who she saw sitting and waiting. It was Detective Jackson, and he was looking good enough to eat. Nala hadn't had sex in a long time, and it was starting to get to her. Although killing was gratifying, there's nothing like the feel of a good, hard, big dick to take the stress away. She missed the intimacy, the kissing, the lovemaking and the sometimes-good raw sex. The kind where the hair is being pulled and the ass is being smacked until it's raw. She missed the feel of a man's body on top of hers, in the back of her, on the side of her and her favorite, head between the legs. One thing about Kendrick she had to admit she missed was the sex, but more so the oral sex. He had the best lick and suck game she had ever experienced. Sometimes, if he didn't give her the dick, she was fine. His licking and the big orgasm that followed would put her out for the night like they had just had a round in the bed. But those days were over. Men to her right now were the enemy, no matter how fine they were.

As Nala walked towards her office, Detective Jackson stood to greet her. She put on an extra switch to her walk because she knew he was feeling her. After all, what else would get him to come out to her job at the beck of a stupid little whore like Crystal. That had to be why he was there, but she would wait and hear it from him.

"Good morning Dr. Jordan. I would have called your phone to inform you of your guest, but I knew class was ending for you, and he just got here."

"No problem," she said, unlocking the office door.

"Good morning, Dr. Jordan. I hope this isn't a bad time?"

"Well, it's unexpected. What can I do for you?" she said, entering the office with Detective Jackson following her.

"I uh, received a phone call from Ms. Carter. She stated this morning you threatened her life and the life of her unborn baby. Is that true?

Nala chuckled as she turned on her computer screen. It gave her extreme pleasure knowing Crystal was shook. However, she was starting to get pissed at the attention. It didn't look good for a detective to be showing up at her office, no matter how minor it was. If it wasn't Detective Chase, she didn't need the hassle of any other police officer.

"With all due respect, don't you have better things to do with your time? Are you going to jump at every little bump and bruise Ms. Carter says she has? I mean, I thought we were done with her the first time she accused me of doing something to her. She's calling you at every beck and call. Can I file a complaint for harassment"?

"If you feel you are unjustly being accused, then yes, you can file a complaint."

"No, unlike Ms. Carter, I don't have time for games. Listen, I went over to that side of campus today to meet with someone editing my next book. While there I ran into the man who is still my husband and we talked. She didn't like it, so she wanted to play as if she had some leverage."

"Leverage?"

"Yes, leverage. You see, Detective Jackson, the only reason I can think my soon-to-be-ex is marrying her is that she's pregnant. I doubt there's any love there, so her playing like she has the role of the missus, which comes with leverage, is beyond me."

"Oh, I thought they were engaged?"

"Formalities. Anyway, she called you, and your reason for this visit is what?"

"Ms. Carter has filed a restraining order against you, and I'm here to serve it."

He handed Nala the restraining order as her body started to feel like it was on fire. She opened the letter and began reading. Nala was furious. How could that little bitch get a restraining order? She tossed it on the desk, took a deep breath and smiled. Detective Jackson looked at her and smiled back.

"Okay, please explain this to me. She gets a restraining order where I'm not supposed to be in one thousand feet of her. So, what happens if I need to go on that side of campus for business or *pleasure* and I run into her. Then what?"

"I guess you didn't see that stipulation in there. You can encounter her on the premises of your employment, but there always must be a third party involved as a witness. A third party, however, on her part. So, if she sees you, she can go and get someone to be in her presence as a witness if something were to transpire."

"Okay, I'll play her game, for now. She wants to feel in control. She got it. So, if that's all, I do have some business to attend to before the morning is over." She stood up.

"Yes, that's it. Look, I'm sure, once she has the baby, she won't have time for much of anything else. Things should go back to normal by then. Maybe she's just feeling really hormonal right now."

"Hormonal. Right. Okay, well, I can't say it was a pleasure."

"It's always a pleasure."

The two looked at each other for a few seconds before Detective Jackson turned to walk to the door. Nala felt a rush of butterflies in her stomach. Although he was married, there was something about him she really liked.

"If you need anything, don't hesitate to call," he said, extending his hand.

"I won't. Have a good day."

"You too."

Nala sat behind her desk and thought about how to get Crystal back. She couldn't believe the nerve of her getting a restraining order. Nala picked up her phone and looked at the text message from Kendrick she had received earlier. She could play him like a violin if she wanted. It was obvious he realized his mistake and still wanted her. Nala thought to herself how she could use it to her advantage. She texted him, "Are you busy?" and waited for a response.

Within seconds her phone chimed with a message and it read, "No, what's up?"

*What's up?* Nala said to herself. He was the one who wanted her to call. Once again, it was all about control or him believing he had it. So, to give him that idea for the moment, she responded, "You wanted me to call or text."

Kendrick's heart was pounding as he was trying to play it cool. He wanted to desperately say, I want to see you, I miss you, I love you, and I fucked up, but he couldn't. He had to save face. Kendrick sat for about a minute and texted, "Yeah, I did say that. Are you busy later today? I want to talk to you."

Nala, thinking how she could play on his vulnerability, responded, "No, what's up?" Now, the ball was back in his court. He was either going to play or go home, as the NBA says.

He responded, "Can we meet for drinks and talk? Anywhere you want to meet is cool."

Nala sat and thought about it. She didn't want to meet him at a bar or restaurant. She didn't think he would truly let his guard down and open up for fear of possibly running into Crystal. Nala wanted to fuck with him, and she knew just the place she could. The place they once called their home. She knew if she could get him to feel comfortable and unscripted, it would be home. Nala smiled as she texted back, saying, "How about my house? I'm not up for the bar or restaurant scene. I can drink at home."

Kendrick's heart began to pound louder, harder and faster. The last time he had been *home* was unannounced, and it didn't go over so well. Hopefully, the invitation tonight would bring a different vibe. "Okay, cool, what time?"

Nala responded, "6. C u then." She set the phone down and laughed. Kendrick was going to be in for several surprises. The biggest, meeting Dominique.

***

When Nala and Jessica arrived at the police station, Detective Chase was waiting for them in the room deemed the Lady Ice Room. Bryce's picture had been added to the list of murdered men on the wall. Jessica was in awe. She had never been that up close and personal to a murder investigation. It was exciting and adrenaline-rushing at the same time. This was what she hoped to do for a living. For some, it may seem strange to look at dead bodies and examine the minds of serial killers, but for Jessica, it was her calling.

With all the excitement of the morning, Nala realized she hadn't called Dominique. She excused herself from Detective Chase and Jessica and went into the hallway. She dialed the number, and Dominique answered after the second ring.

"Hey, Nala. How's everything? I'm surprised you're just calling me."

"This was actually the only time I had since getting to work. Long story, and I'll fill you in when I get home. How are you? Are you okay? Did you eat?"

"I'm fine, Nala. Yes, I'm okay, and yes, I ate. For breakfast, I had a boiled egg, toast and coffee. For lunch, I had a salad with a glass of water. I'm good."

"Did you talk to Mom?"

"Yes, I did. We had a wonderful talk. I'm surprised she didn't call you."

"Actually, she did, but it's been busy and crazy today. Like I said, we'll talk. I'm at the police station working on the case. I'll be home shortly."

"Okay. See you soon."

"Okay, bye."

Nala ended the call and returned to the room with Detective Chase and Jessica. She sat her purse down and walked over to the "wall of horrors." That was her work. That was her anger. Sometimes, she couldn't believe she had actually killed someone, seven people to be exact. Seven men were dead, and the police were clueless. Was she actually that good? Looking at her work gave her a rush. She didn't know if the rush was from being excited or being shocked. Whatever it was, it made her woozy. Detective Chase noticed her stumble backward.

When the Heart Turns Cold 3

"Are you okay, Dr. Jordan?" he asked, walking over to her and putting his hand on her back for support.

"Yes, I'm fine. Just got a little lightheaded," she said, sitting down.

"Yeah, well, I can understand that. Even for the most seasoned detective, you never get used to seeing images like these."

"Are you okay, Dr. Jordan?" asked a concerned Jessica.

"Yes. Honestly, the pictures don't bother me. I haven't eaten today. It has been a long and strange day. I just need to get home," she said, looking at Jessica for her to begin. "So, Jessica, if you could tell Detective Chase why you're here."

"Okay. Well, for my class with Dr. Jordan, I've been assigned the Lady Ice case. So, I'm out for dinner last week and I bump right into the murder victim, Bryce Wilkins. He was at the Indian restaurant downtown."

"Are you sure it was him?" Detective Chase asked excitedly.

"Yes. But that's not the clincher. The reason I bumped into him was that he was rushing behind a woman. A woman with long black hair and wearing dark shades. If I had to guess, I would say it was Lady Ice."

"Well, did you get a good look at her?"

"No, not really. She was quick. To be honest, she looked like she was spooked. Like maybe she saw someone she didn't want to see."

"Wow, this is good. So, after you bumped into Mr. Wilkins, what happened?"

135

"Well, he bent down to pick up my keys because he knocked them out of my hand when he ran into me. He apologized and hurried after the lady."

"Did you see a car they were driving, anything?"

"No, I'm sorry. After I took my keys, I followed the waitress to be seated."

"Okay, okay. I want you to work with our sketch artist and tell him as much as you can remember about what she looked like, what she wore, anything. Hopefully, this will be the break we need to catch this woman."

Detective Chase left the room while Jessica and Nala sat silent. Nala was trying to recall if there was anything in particular that had her stand out that day. She wore her wig and shades but nothing else to camouflage her appearance. She hoped there was nothing Jessica could remember that would bring them to her.

When the sketch artist arrived, he and Jessica began while Nala stood up and walked over to photos again. Detective Chase walked over to her and stood beside her. He crossed his arms as he sighed out loudly.

"You know, any murder is one too many, but when she killed one of our own, it became personal. We used to call Friscoe "Rags" because he always carried a rag around to wipe the sweat off his forehead. Even in the Winter, he sweat," he laughed. "He was a good officer and a good man, and we miss him. She has to pay for that."

"Good man? Um, if he was with Lady Ice, he was cheating."

"Okay, so he had his shortcomings. Is that grounds for murder? Heck, if our shortcomings were grounds for murder, we'd all be dead. What shortcoming would kill you, Dr. Jordan?"

Nala looked at him and grinned. *If only he knew,* she thought to herself. Nala turned her attention to Jessica. It seemed as if they were finishing up as Nala and Detective Chase walked over to them. Nala glimpsed at the sketch and thought to herself that Jessica remembered more than she thought. It was a pretty good sketch. Actually, it was damn good. Nala walked away and sat down, not wanting to bring any attention from the photo to her. In the blink of an eye, they could look at it and think it resembled her. She didn't need that to happen.

"So, what we'll do is send this to the news stations again and the newspapers. Someone must know this woman. She can't be that off the radar. So, Dr. Jordan. The last time I asked did you think she was done or would kill again, you weren't sure. And low and behold, she kills Mr. Wilkins that night. Coincidence or what?"

"I don't know. All I do is profile. I can't guarantee a hundred percent."

"So, if you had to profile this perp again, what would it be?"

"The same as before. Nothing's changed. I don't know if she is done or truly just getting started."

"Seven men dead. She needs to be done and caught!"

"I understand your frustration but..."

"With all due respect, Dr. Jordan, you don't. For everyone else, this is just a news story. When it's first told, people are in shock and disbelief, maybe even angry. But after a few days, they forget. But not the victim's family. They never forget. They want justice, so they call each and every day asking if there are any leads, did we catch her yet? Then, they get frustrated and say we aren't doing our jobs. When the world forgets, we don't, and neither do their families. I'm beyond frustrated when I have a victim and the person responsible is walking free."

"I'm sorry. I didn't mean any disrespect. I've worked many cases where I see how personal it becomes for law enforcement. It is hard not to get frustrated and angry. I get it."

"I know you do, and I didn't mean to take it out on you."

"I know and we're good." She smiled. "Let's just hope she disappears and never murders again."

"For her not to murder again, I want her caught and strapped to a gurney."

Nala nodded her head in agreement as Jessica stood to the side, listening. She was happy to be a part of what she hoped would be a ground-breaking case. The sketch artist left the room as they sat down to discuss the case more. Jessica pulled out her notes, and Detective Chase was impressed. He saw a bright future for her. After an hour of looking over the case file and other information, they called it quits. Detective Chase needed to get prepared for his spot on the news with the photo once again.

When Nala and Jessica got outside, Jessica decided to hang around in the city for a while. She told Nala she didn't need a ride back to campus. Nala couldn't put her finger on it, but something seemed different about Jessica since leaving the precinct. She felt every time she turned away Jessica was staring at her. Was it possible she could see the resemblance between her and Lady Ice? Nala had to find out, but she had to do it delicately. After all, killing Jessica was not an option, but making her disappear could be.

***

Nala arrived home within an hour of leaving the precinct. She knew she would miss the first news broadcast of Detective Chase, but she would catch it at 11 p.m. Kendrick had texted her, making sure they were still on, and her mother had phoned her again a couple of times. She had to call her back, but she needed to handle Kendrick and talk to Dominique.

When Nala walked inside the house, Dominique met her with a glass of red wine. She took Nala's briefcase and pocketbook and sat them on the table. Nala smiled as they walked into the living room. She sat down and put her feet up on the coffee table as Dominque sat next to her. It felt good to relax. She needed to get her head in check before Kendrick arrived. Nala sipped on her wine and tried to figure out where to begin telling her mother the events of the day. She decided from the beginning would be the best. However, before she started her rant, she wanted to know how the conversation went between her and her mother.

"So, was Mom happy to hear from you?"

"Yes, she was, and I was happy to talk to her. It's been a long time."

"Yeah, I know. I'm glad y'all talked. She called me several times, but I didn't get a chance to get back to her. I'll call her before I go to bed. I want her and Dad to come for the weekend anyway to see you. I think that would be nice."

139

"It sure would be. I missed my sister. Thirty-plus years is a long time not to see your loved ones. It's way overdue. So, how was your day?"

"Well," she said, finishing her wine in her glass. "I had a visit from the police at the request of Crystal. She has a restraining order against me."

"Really? Why?"

"This morning, I went over to the side of the campus where she and Kendrick work, and I ran into him. We talked for a while, and then she appeared. Of course, she didn't like us talking, and she flipped out. I put her back in her place, and she felt threatened. So, the little bitch, excuse my language, calls the detective she sicked on me before and took out a restraining order."

"And what did your husband say?"

"He tried to appease both sides, but I wasn't having it. I ripped her, then I walked away."

"So, how much longer are you planning to put up with this mess? It's evident she needs to be taught a serious lesson that will have her so shook she'll think the devil was behind it."

"And he may be. But I got something up my sleeve. Speaking of my husband, you'll get a chance to meet him tonight. He'll be here, actually, in about an hour."

"Ohhhh, so I get to meet the man behind the hate, huh? Good."

***

Nala had another drink with her mother before going upstairs to take a shower and change. She put on a pair of sweat shorts, which were tight and fitting to her curves, and

140

a tank top. She knew Kendrick loved when she dressed that way. He thought she looked sexy and raw, and it always got him rock hard and ready to fuck. That was the outcome she was going for. Nala went downstairs into the living room and turned on the music. When her mother saw her outfit, she smiled and shook her head. She knew what it meant. As Nala lit a few candles, the doorbell rang. Her mother sat down and crossed her legs with an almost sinister look on her face. Nala perked up her breast, moistened her lips and walked to the door and opened it. Kendrick tried not to look like he was drooling, but she could see the dog in him.

"Right on time, come in?" she said.

Kendrick walked in and stood at the door. He couldn't help but stare at her. She looked good to him. Nala looked down at his crotch to see if she could see his manhood rising, and he was still asleep, but not for long. She thought to herself how fun it was going to be to play him tonight.

"So, how were you able to get away from *Crystal*?"

"I told her I needed to take care of some things, nothing major."

"Mmm-hmmm. Same thing you used to tell me, huh? Well, luckily that's not my problem anymore. She got it. So, you wanted to talk. What's up?"

"Can we go and sit down in the living room or wherever?"

"Let's go in the living room. I have someone I'd like you to meet anyway."

Kendrick looked puzzled as he followed her into the living room. Dominique was still sitting in her same position on the chair. When Kendrick entered the room, she tried not to look how she felt. After all, he was the man who woke up the demon in Nala that was planted by her and Robert. Dominique believed it would have remained dormant had Nala not gone through all the emotional drama. Dominique knew those feelings all too well. After killing her bully when she was a child, the sense of wanting to kill went to sleep, and it remained asleep until she murdered her husband and his friends.

At times, she was thankful for being locked up. She often wondered what she would have become if not caught. Would the bitterness have consumed her like it did Nala, and she resorted to killing? She knew what her daughter was responsible for. Her pretty, little innocent girl who she had to leave when she was five years old. At times, when Dominique looked at her, that's who she saw. Not a murderer or a woman who had brutally killed seven men.

"Kendrick, I want you to meet my mother, Ms. Richards."

"Um, nice to meet you," he said, shaking her hand and looking perplexed.

"So, you're Kendrick. My daughter's husband. The one who broke her heart?"

Kendrick's head lowered in shame as he didn't know how to answer that. He knew he messed up big time and hurt Nala. He felt bad about that and wanted to fix the huge mistake he made. That what he was hoping to do tonight.

"Yes, ma'am, I'm guilty as charged for hurting Nala, and I hope to fix it. But, uh, Nala, this is your *mother*?"

"Yes, I am, and I'm sure she'll fill you in later but getting back to you. Did you not know the jewel you were married to? What would make you hurt such a delicate gem?"

"Um, I guess I just got caught up."

"Caught up, huh?' Dominique chuckled. "Well, how do you like the outcome of getting caught up?"

"I don't."

Dominique stood up and walked over to Kendrick. She looked him over for a few seconds then looked at Nala. She wanted to say so much, but she knew things were handled if she knew her daughter.

"Let me give you a word of advice, young man. There are plenty of sad, lonely and divorced men who got *caught up*. Be careful of what you're allowing to catch you because it could wind up being the end of you, literally. Nala, I'm going to my room."

"Okay. See you later."

Dominique walked away, and Kendrick and Nala sat down. Nala could tell Kendrick was confused with a lot of questions, but tonight wasn't about Dominique. It was about her breaking him. Nala hadn't looked at Kendrick in an admiring way in a long time, but, with a few glasses of wine she had before he arrived, he was looking good to her. He actually had her feeling horny and warm all over. It was cool because she knew if she allowed him to have her, that the feeling would be gone, and she would go back to despising him completely.

"So, you wanted to talk. What's up?"

"Listen, Nala, I'm not going to act as if I was the best man you ever had in your life, but I know I wasn't the worst. I made mistakes, quite a few, but I never stopped loving you. That never changed."

"So, if I'm to understand what you're saying, you cheat on me three times, screw other women, one in my bed, I may add, and loving me never changed? How's that possible?"

"Because I didn't love them, I loved, love you. I'm not going to sit here and blame anyone for my shortcomings. I cheated because I wanted to. It had nothing to do with what you were or weren't doing. You were the best thing to ever happen to me. I mean, what man wouldn't want you? It was me and my dumb ass. All I know is I made a colossal mistake, and I'm sorry. I'm sorry for all the hurt, the pain, the doubts, the anger and anything else you had to feel because of my actions. I'm so sorry, Nala, and I need you to forgive me. Please."

"Why do you need my forgiveness? You have what you want. A fiancé whose about to have your child. A child we talked about having to build our family but never did. Why Kendrick, do you *need* my forgiveness? To ease your conscience? To make things better for you? Why?"

"Because I still love you, and I want you back. I want our marriage back. The one before the bullshit. The good one. The one where we couldn't wait to get home to make love to each other. The one where making love lasted all day. The one, baby, where you felt safe with me and in my arms. I want that marriage back."

For a split second, Nala believed him. His voice sounded sincere, and he looked remorseful. Was he really sorry or just fed up with Crystal? He had a lot riding with her, the biggest being she was pregnant. It didn't matter how sorry he was or how badly he wanted her back; there was no going back for her. It was too late, and too much had happened. She was Lady Ice, serial killer of seven men. Her life now was anything but normal. There was no room for Kendrick for anything serious. However, if she wanted to, she could make him her toy to play with when she got the urge to be fucked. Fucking didn't entail emotions. A person could be as detached as they needed. In her thinking, men did it all the time.

Nala got up and went to sit next to Kendrick. She could tell he was nervous by his chest heaving up and down. He looked like a virgin about to get some ass. She had him now, and anything she wanted from him she knew she could get. Nala put her hand on his leg and looked him in the eyes. Kendrick slowly put his hand over hers and smiled. This was the moment when he would take a chance that would get him slapped or get him back the woman he loved.

Nala felt he was about to go in for the kill and kiss her. Although her heart was cold as ice for him, her body was on fire. Sex sounded like a good plan at that moment. Kendrick reached over and kissed her once. His lips felt like silk as Nala felt her pussy throbbing and getting wet. Since there was no resistance, he reached over again, but he kissed her with passion this time. Their tongues did a dance as they kissed and held each other. It definitely felt good to both of them. Kendrick began licking her ear and whispering how much he loved her. Nala felt herself getting lost in the feeling as she held him tight and accepted all his affection. She had forgotten how it felt to be loved by Kendrick, and for a split second, it felt good. But Nala knew this wasn't about rekindling old feelings. It was about her getting Crystal back. Nala pulled away from Kendrick and moved over to the sofa. She looked down at his crotch and bingo.

His dick was rock hard and standing at attention. She turned away and smiled and then looked back at him.

"What's wrong?" he asked.

"You know there is no way Crystal is giving you up, right?"

"It's not her choice if I don't want to be there."

"Did you know she got a restraining order against me today?" Nala asked as she got up and walked over to the minibar to pour herself a glass of red wine.

"What? No, I didn't know. Why she do that?"

"Well, according to little Ms. Drama Queen, she felt threatened by me this morning. Detective Jackson served me the papers at work today. Do you know how embarrassing that was? I have been a respected and valuable employee at Woodson, and that was so unacceptable," she said, drinking her wine.

"You damn right it was. That wasn't cool. Okay, listen, I'll handle it. I promise."

Kendrick got up and walked over to Nala. He took the glass of wine from her hand and reached down and kissed her again as they both slowly backed up against the fireplace. Kendrick looked down at her and softly gripped her ass. He began pulling down her shorts and was excited to find she didn't have any panties. Kendrick kneeled in front of her and raised her leg over his shoulder. Nala looked down at him with a smile and anticipation for what was to come. Kendrick began kissing her inner thighs and licking them. His tongue felt warm as it made its way to her wet clitoris. Kendrick licked it, then sucked it. He remembered how Nala loved to hear him slurp her juices as they began to flow. Nala began to moan like a cat in heat while Kendrick ran his tongue over her clit and in and out of her pussy. She held his head firmly, ensuring he wouldn't stop. Kendrick gripped her ass close to his face so she could experience every lick and stroke with full force. Nala's hips swayed with his tongue as she moaned louder and held his head harder.

"Yes, Kendrick, yes! Suck this pussy," she moaned. "Tell me who you love," she asked.

"I love you, baby," he said, coming up for air.

Nala felt herself about to have the biggest orgasm she'd had in a while, but she didn't want to cum that way. She pushed his head back, and Kendrick looked startled as he stood up.

"What's wrong?" he asked.

"Fuck me," she replied.

Kendrick unzipped his pants and pulled them down along with his underwear. He stepped out of them and turned Nala around facing the fireplace. She arched her back, stuck out her ass and put her leg up on the chair. Kendrick stood behind her and entered her delicately. He held her waist firmly as his dick went in and out of her. Her pussy was so wet that it made a popping sound that turned them on with each stroke.

"Who you love, Kendrick, who?" Nala asked.

"You baby, you," he grunted.

"Say my name," she demanded.

"Nala, mmm. Nala, shit, you feel so fucking good. You always had the best pussy, girl," he said, stroking her.

Nala bent over more and spread her ass cheeks so she could have all of him. "I'm cumming," she moaned as her body went into spasm.

Kendrick pulled her closer to him as he came with her. The two moaned and grunted in sync as their bodies went through an orgasmic euphoria. Nala's leg began to shake as she took it off the chair. Kendrick smiled at his work.

"Damn, girl. It's been a long time, right?"

"Yeah, it has. You can go to the bathroom and clean yourself up. You know where it is."

Kendrick picked up his clothes and quickly headed to the bathroom. Nala walked over to the sofa and put back on her shorts. She poured herself another glass of wine and drank it down. A nice, hot shower would top off the night. Kendrick had come back within ten minutes. He walked over to Nala and gave her a kiss. She wasn't as receptive as earlier. After all, she had got fucked good, and she was fine. For her, things were back to normal.

"What's wrong?" Kendrick asked.

"Nothing. I'm just tired, that's all. Been a long day. I think I'm going to take a shower and turn in," she said, getting up and walking to the front door.

"Oh damn, it's like that? Put the money on the nightstand before you bounce type thing, huh?"

"What did you expect it to be? Listen, the sex was always good between us, but right now, that's all it is...sex."

"I was hoping for it to be more."

"Kendrick, you have a bit of a dilemma named Crystal. Whatever you're hoping to happen between us can't with her in the picture. That's just how it is."

"I can leave her. That's not a problem."

"Do you really think leaving her would work? I'm here to tell you it won't. Shit, for a chick like that, you'd have to kill her," Nala said, chuckling.

Nala opened the front door, and Kendrick stepped out. He turned around to face her. She looked so damn good to him. He wanted her back badly, but he did know Crystal wouldn't go away freely. He did have a problem, but he was willing to give it a shot, whatever it took to solve it.

"Can I call you tomorrow," he asked.

"How about I call you?"

"Are you going to call, Nala?" he asked with concern.

"Yeah, I will. Okay.

"Alright. Talk to you then."

"Mmm-hmm, okay."

Kendrick turned and walked away as Nala closed the door. She was surprised to see Dominique standing there. Nala crossed her arms and leaned against the door.

"Someone once told me that sex is just as lethal as any weapon you can use to kill someone. Do you agree with that?" Nala said with a menacing smile.

"That's what I've been told."

Dominique laughed as she walked away. Nala had Kendrick right where she wanted him. If anything, she knew sex, especially good sex, could make a man crumble and do anything a woman asked of him. Powerful men were weakened, and cities have fallen because of a woman and her good sex. That was where she had Kendrick, and she was pleased.

## Chapter 13

When Nala awoke that morning, she had several texts from Kendrick. She read them and tossed her phone on the bed as she stretched. She didn't have time to think about Kendrick. Her dream from last night had her thoughts preoccupied. She sat up in the bed and looked around the room. Nala hadn't felt that uneasy since the dreams when there was banging on her door. If she believed Dominique, which she thought she had no choice, then she had to believe it was Randstad saying his goodbyes. Last night's dream felt that way. Dreaming about her father spooked her. She didn't want him invading her dreams or thoughts. Nala got out of bed and went into the bathroom to brush her teeth. She needed to speak with Dominique to get her interpretations. When she opened her bedroom door, she could smell the aroma of coffee and bacon. Nala smiled as she headed downstairs into the kitchen. Dominique had the table set for two as she stood at the stove flipping bacon. There was fresh fruit on the table along with cream cheese and bagels.

"Smells good," Nala said as she sat down and ate two grapes.

"Oh, hey. Didn't hear you come in." Dominique took the bacon off the grill, putting it on a plate and sitting it on the table. She then went to the oven and took out a plate that had two vegetable omelets on it. Nala was pleased. Dominique sat down and placed one of the omelets on Nala's plate as Nala took a few pieces of bacon.

"This looks good. What do you have in this omelet?"

"Sun-dried tomatoes, mushrooms, spinach and cheese."

"Oh wow, I had all that in my fridge?" she asked, taking a piece.

"Yes, you did," she said, laughing.

"It's really good. I can get used to this again. Kendrick always cooked for me. He was pretty good too."

"There's nothing sexier than a man who can cook. So, did you accomplish what you set out to last night?

"Oh yes, better than I expected."

"Whatever you're up to, play your cards carefully. A person in love with a broken heart can be dangerous. You should know that."

"Oh, I'm good. I have everything under control. Crystal and Kendrick haven't seen my wrath yet. But enough about them, for now. I had a dream about Robert last night."

"A dream, huh? No, it wasn't a dream. He came to visit you. What did he say?"

"He asked if I was done yet. He asked how did it feel to have killed just as many people as he had. He wanted to know how it felt to be his daughter and to have the same blood flowing through me that ran through him."

"And how did you answer him?"

"I said it feels like it did the last time I saw him in jail. It feels sickening."

"You still think you're so different than him, don't you?"

"I am."

"And why is that? Because somehow, you've justified your killings? You think you're righting the wrongs of all married women who have been hurt by their husbands? Is that it?"

"Well, yeah. I didn't kill for the hell of it like he did. I killed because those men deserved it."

"And Robert thought those women deserved it. Now what?"

"I really can't believe you still defend him after what he did. How do you do it?"

"Because like I told you, I didn't know that Robert and because I loved him, just like I love you. I haven't turned my back on you, and you've done some horrific things. You've murdered too, brutally. You left wives and children without their loved ones, too. You're no different than him or me. We're all murderers. The only difference is you haven't been caught to pay for your crimes. I hope you never are."

"Well, Mom, I'm not him."

"Are you done righting those wrongs? Because if I had to guess, I don't think you are. I think you're like a hound dog who has gotten a taste for blood. You crave it. Are you done killing, my sweet Daisy?"

"It's not about me right now. We're talking about Robert. And please don't call me Daisy."

"Okay, we're talking about Robert. What else did he reveal or say?"

"Before I woke up, he said the name Lauren Price. That's it."

Dominique turned as pale as a white sheet. It was as if all the blood had drained from her face. She picked up her coffee and drank some of it. Nala could tell she was trying to compose herself. Now, Dominque was spooked. What did the name mean? Who was she?

"Does that name mean anything to you?"

"Um, no," she said, clearing her throat. "Not at all."

"Are you okay?" Nala asked.

"Yes, I'm okay. So, do you work today?"

"Yeah. I actually need to go and get myself together. Thanks for breakfast." Nala got up from the table. "Uh, do you mind taking care of the dishes?"

"Of course not. Go get ready for work."

"Okay."

Dominique sat at the table and finished her coffee feeling very nervous. One thing she thought she had going for her was Nala not believing that Randstad was visiting her in her dreams. Hopefully, she would continue to not believe it and not look into who Lauren was.

***

When Nala got to work, she sat behind her desk and turned on the computer. She had no class today, but she had an awful lot of work to do. She needed to go over some edits for her second book and work on her plan to get Crystal back. Nala dug her cell phone out of her purse and texted Kendrick, asking him to come and see her if he had time. She knew he would come running like a lost dog. Within seconds, he responded he would be there this morning. Nala smiled as she sat her phone on the desk and looked at the screen on the computer. She immediately thought back to her conversation with Dominique this morning and how she reacted to Lauren Price's name. Nala pulled up Google and entered the name in the search engine. She was shocked to see there was actually a person named Lauren Price. She thought it was just a dream and the ramblings of a dead man and love-struck woman talking. Nala clicked on one of the news stories, and a picture accompanied the article. The picture was that of a young black girl who looked to be in her early twenties. Under the picture read, "No leads in the death of college junior Lauren Price." Nala's mouth dropped as she began to read the article. It stated how Lauren's body was found in an abandoned warehouse near some train tracks. She had been strangled. There were several leads, but none promising enough to arrest and convict someone. As Nala continued to read, she couldn't believe what she came across. The victim had interned in Dominique's law firm, and when asked how she felt about the murder, she replied, "It's a travesty. Lauren was a bright girl with a promising future. The world has lost a jewel."

Nala sat back in her chair with her mouth still open. She couldn't believe her dream revealed something real from a serial killer who happened to be her father. She began to feel freaked out. He was truly entering her dreams and talking to her. It almost felt like some Freddy Krueger shit. What was next? Would he start to invade her world now? What was even more alarming was her mother knew something about the Lauren girl, and she also knew about Robert making contact from the dead. Were they witches or something? Did they practice black magic? Nala had a ton of questions as her head was spinning with thoughts. She printed the story and looked it over once more, particularly the picture of Lauren. She was a beautiful young girl who reminded Nala of herself. Why would someone kill her? From the news article, she was a well-liked girl with a bright future in law. It was puzzling, and Nala promised to find out first thing when she got home.

Nala began to scroll through her email and came across one from Crystal. She was surprised because of the nature of their relationship. The subject line read: "Baby Shower Announcement." Nala chuckled and said, "this bitch," as she opened the email. There was a picture of her and Kendrick with him rubbing her belly. She clicked on the audio button, and Crystal said, "One heart, plus two hearts make three hearts. Please join Kendrick and me as we celebrate our new bundle of God's blessing. We are both so excited and look forward to sharing this milestone in our lives with you." Below the picture was the shower information and where they were registered. Nala couldn't believe the audacity of Crystal. Although the email had been sent before she took out the restraining order, she felt like she still had a lot of nerve. But Nala knew the game. Once again, Crystal felt like she needed to be a priority. Nala laughed as she thought about Kendrick's head buried in her pussy last night. If only Crystal knew the one she was trying to be a priority for was making someone else his. Nala continued looking through her emails as she looked up and saw Kendrick walking towards her office. He stopped in front of her secretary's desk. She buzzed Nala, and Nala told her to send him in.

"Have a seat," Nala said, pointing to the chair.

"You know, I couldn't get you off my mind last night, right?"

"I tend to have that effect on people. So, did you get in trouble last night when you got home? I'm sure the Mrs. was up and waiting patiently."

"No, everything was cool."

"Well, I really don't care. You're a big boy. However, what I do care about is this invite to your baby shower. Your little girl sure she wants me to come? I mean, she might be biting off more than she can chew by inviting me. She may think it's a joke, and I may think it's not."

"Um, I'm sure that was a mistake on her part. Actually, one of her friends sent out an email blast to all her friends in her contacts. She must not have removed you."

"Ohhhh, pity," she said sarcastically. "I was looking forward to coming. So, are you excited about being a daddy?"

Kendrick lowered his eyes from Nala in remorse. They talked about having children many times. That was one of the reasons they purchased the big house in Media. It was a nice, quiet area with a good school district, and it felt like a safe place to raise a family. Although Kendrick knew he hurt Nala tremendously with his infidelity, he never wanted to hurt her in that way. Getting Crystal pregnant was not part of the plan. It was a mistake he regretted but one he couldn't change. As much as Nala acted as if Crystal being pregnant didn't bother her, he knew it did. After all, he knew Nala very well. He could tell with her gestures, tones and looks when she was angry, hurt or sad. The topic of Crystal being pregnant hurt her.

"I'm as excited as I should be, I guess."

"You guess? Come on, Kendrick, you're about to be a daddy. Something you've always wanted. You should be ecstatic!" she said sarcastically.

"Let talk about something else. Like, how can we fix things?"

"Well, Kendrick, fixing things entails a lot."

"Like what? Tell me."

"Actually, Kendrick, to be honest, I don't think I could deal with you having a child. That's a bit much."

'There's nothing I can do about the kid, but if we got back together, it would more than likely live with Crystal. I would just have visitation, so having it wouldn't be full-time. We could talk about when I get the kid and for how long. Anything to not make you uncomfortable."

"*It*, wow, Kendrick. That's how you refer to your child?" she grinned.

"No, I didn't mean, look, I never wanted this. I never asked to be a dad with Crystal. I always wanted children with you, my wife. Getting her pregnant was a huge mistake, one I'm paying for now. But we can make it work. I know we can. If we get back together, I promise you, I will make things right."

"Okay, Kendrick, it's a lot to think about. I need time. I mean, there's a baby on the way, and you're about to get married again soon and…"

"The only person I'm hoping to marry again soon is you. But we can call off the divorce, then I can't get remarried."

Nala folded her hands and thought about that. Even though she didn't want to stay married to Kendrick, if she did, Crystal couldn't have him as her husband. It sounded like a good plan, for now. She would call off the divorce, and, when she finished destroying them, she would refile. She looked at Kendrick, smiled and said, "Call your lawyer. There's no divorce happening between the Jordan's."

Kendrick clapped his hands loudly and laughed out a robust laugh. Nala had made him a happy man. He wanted to kiss her, but he knew he couldn't. However, Nala was thinking differently. She stood up and walked over to him. Nala kneeled and kissed him on the lips. Her secretary, who was returning from the bathroom, saw it and turned away quickly.

"Okay, so I'll call my lawyer this morning, and you call yours. Maybe we can meet for drinks later and discuss what's next," Nala said, walking to the office door.

Kendrick got up feeling like the luckiest man in the world. For now, there would be no divorce, and he was happy with that. "Okay, I'll call him as soon as I get back to my office. I promise you, Nala, I will never hurt you again. I swear, baby. I love you."

"I love you too."

Kendrick reached over and kissed her on the lips, then he walked out. Nala closed the door and went to sit back down. She despised him even more because there was no ounce of loyalty in his body. He was willing to throw his unborn child under the bus just to make her happy. What man does that? But, whatever the case, it wasn't her problem. Their bastard child, their relationship based on lies and deceit, and Kendrick still being an ass was what it was all about. Nala buzzed her secretary for some coffee as she opened her notes to edit her book. Today was an office hour day and she had a few appointments scheduled with her students.

While she looked over her schedule, her secretary brought her in a cup of coffee. She considered Nala a great boss and a good friend; however, she knew Nala's personal life was hers. She couldn't help but see her kiss Kendrick, and she was curious. It was all a part of Nala's plan. She hoped if Kendrick was seen in her office one too many times, it would eventually get back to Crystal. Nala knew her secretary wanted to ask her about Kendrick, but she didn't know how. So, to make her feel as if she wasn't prying, Nala gave her what she wanted.

"I know you saw Kendrick and I kiss, and you're probably wondering what's the deal. Well, we're trying to figure that out too. We're taking it slow, you know what I mean?"

"Dr. Jordan, I didn't want to seem like I was snooping or anything, but I haven't seen that in a long time. You and Professor Jordan were like Barack and Michelle around here until you broke up. Whatever the case, I wish you well. You deserve to be happy."

"Thank you. I appreciate it."

She walked out of the office with a smile as Nala got back to her work. She felt it only a matter of time before people would notice Kendrick's frequent appearances in her office, and that's what she was hoping.

*** 

Crystal was quiet on the ride home. She couldn't figure out why Kendrick was so happy. She hoped it was because they were having a baby soon, but she wasn't sure. Although she hadn't said anything last night, she noticed the time he came home. It wasn't extremely late, but he hadn't said anything to her when he got in. In her book, those were red flags. Crystal knew she could get paranoid easily about her man, so instead of guessing, she would just ask any questions she wanted answers to.

"So, you're in a good mood. What's up?" she asked.

"Nothing, life is just good, that's all."

"I hope that's because we're in it," she said, rubbing her belly.

"Yeah, yeah, it is," he said, looking at her.

"Um, so last night, by the time you got in, I was sleep. Where were you?"

Kendrick looked at her and chuckled. He wasn't going to allow Crystal to pull him into her drama. He was feeling good. Nothing was going to mess up that moment for him. He was on the verge of getting his wife back, and that's all he cared about. He continued to drive and hum a tune that was in his head. Crystal tried not to get angry, but she hated being ignored. She would rather he give her some bullshit answer, but to ignore her was unacceptable. She cleared her throat and turned to look at him. The seat belt felt tight around her neck as she adjusted it to her body.

"Um, did you hear what I asked?"

"Yeah, I did. But if I had to guess, it seems like you're trying to start an argument, and I don't want to argue."

"How am I trying to start an argument by asking my husband where he was last night?"

"Husband? Yo, take a few steps back, girl. We ain't there yet."

"Damn, it's like that now, huh? We're into formalities now? Okay, well, how is asking my *man* where he was is starting an argument?

"Crystal, you were asleep when I got in last night. I didn't want to disturb you because you said you've been tired lately. I thought I was doing something by letting you sleep. I was only looking out for you and the baby. Damn! Damned if I do and damned if I don't."

Crystal looked at Kendrick and felt bad for thinking anything less of him. She wasn't trying to be messy, but she wanted to know where he was. She felt left out with him being quiet and smiling like a cat who just caught a mouse.

"I'm sorry. That was sweet of you. I have been tired lately. With work, planning the shower and planning for a baby, along with a wedding, it's beginning to take a toll."

"Wedding?"

"Yes, wedding. We are getting married, right?"

"Can we please take one major event at a time? Please?" he asked with sarcasm.

"Okay, okay. I just want everything to be right. I love you, baby," she said, rubbing his hand.

Kendrick wanted to desperately pull away, but he had already shown her too much of how he felt. He had to slow down. He didn't want her getting suspicious. His plan was to leave her and move back home. Her touch felt anything but good to him anymore. He longed for Nala's warm body and feel against his. Crystal just didn't compare. Truth be told, she never did, but he was weak. Beautiful, sexy woman flaunting her body in front of him and easily giving up the ass. It was too much for any man to bear. His stepping out on Nala had nothing to do with what she was or wasn't doing. It was all him, and he knew how badly he messed up. Kendrick hoped it wouldn't be long before he was back home, in his bed, with his wife. After he spoke to the lawyer earlier about stopping the divorce proceedings, he felt like he was on his way to being happy again. He wished he could have stayed with Nala tonight, but he knew that couldn't happen.

"I know you do. Just relax. We'll be home soon."

Crystal laid her head back and closed her eyes. She peeped he didn't respond by telling her he loved her as well. But, she wasn't going to say anything, for the moment.

*** 

Nala couldn't wait to get home to confront Dominique about the girl Lauren Price. How could she explain this? Within fifteen minutes, she was pulling into her driveway. She pulled her cell phone out of her pocketbook and called her mother. She had been avoiding her call since she returned from California. It wasn't intentional, or maybe it was. She didn't want her to think she didn't want or need her anymore because that was not true. She was hoping her parents could come for the weekend to spend time with Dominique. Nala speed-dialed her mother, and she answered quickly.

"Hey, Nala. How are you? I feel like we haven't talked in a month of Sundays."

"I know, Mommy, and I'm sorry. Been a little busy with work, the book..."

"Your mother," she softly said.

"Well, yeah, but other things had me busier."

"Nala, it's okay. When we told you about your biological mother, it was a shock. It's no wonder you wanted to find out all you could about her and get to know her. I'm just glad she was finally able to come home, to your home. That's a blessing."

"Yeah, it is, but I don't want you and Dad to feel like I don't need you anymore. I love you guys."

"And we love you too, and we don't feel that way. We're happy for you because we love you. Okay."

"Okay. Well, you're coming this weekend, right? You and Daddy?"

"Of course, we are. I miss my sister very much. We talked for a while today. I can't wait to see her."

"And I can't wait to see you. I miss you and Dad."

"We miss you too."

Nala talked to her mother for about ten minutes before grabbing her purse and briefcase and getting out of the car. She didn't know what to expect from Dominique when she presented to her what she learned. It was becoming all too eerie, and Nala wanted to understand why. She put her key in the door and turned the lock. She heard it click as she opened the door and walked in. The house was quiet, too quiet. She wasn't sure if Dominique was taking a nap or even there. Nala sat her belongings down on the table and walked into the living room. There was no sign of Dominique. She checked the rest of the downstairs and did not see her. The only other place she could be was her bedroom. Nala walked upstairs and knocked on Dominique's door several times.

When there was no answer, she slowly opened the door, just in case she was sleeping. She was surprised to see Dominique not in bed. Nala became worried as she started calling her name. She went back downstairs and walked back to the patio, and still no sign of her. Nala's heart began beating rapidly as her mind raced with thoughts. She quickly walked over to her pocketbook and pulled out her cell, about to dial 911. As her finger started to touch the last number, the doorknob to the front door turned and Dominique walked in dressed in sweats in sneakers. Nala could tell she had been jogging or speed walking from her heavy breathing.

"Hey," she said, panting.

"Hey! Where have you been? I've been worried sick. I looked all over this big house for you, and you weren't here. Where did you go?"

"I went for a joggawalk."

"A who?"

"A joggawalk. That's when you jog some, then walk and walk some, then jog," she said, walking to the kitchen.

"In the future, if you could, please leave a note, a text message, a voicemail, something! I was worried sick."

"Oh, girl, please. Worried sick for what? I can take care of myself. This is a safe neighborhood. Besides, if I can survive thirty-plus years in a mental institution, I can survive a joggawalk," she said, laughing.

"Well, maybe you can, but I can't. Please, just let me know when you feel the need to wander."

"Nala, I'm not a damn child. I don't have to tell you when and where I go. If it's going to be like this living here, then I'll leave. I don't need someone constantly on my back!" she yelled, leaving the kitchen and going upstairs.

Nala stood there with her mouth gaped open. She had no idea where the outburst from Dominique came from. She wanted to follow her upstairs to talk to her, but she decided to give her some space. Nala turned on some jazz music and poured herself a glass of wine. She took the salmon she seasoned last night out of the refrigerator and began to prepare dinner. After about an hour, Dominique came downstairs into the kitchen. Nala had finished making dinner and was sitting and enjoying her wine and the music. She didn't know if she should say anything to Dominique, so she just sat quietly, hoping she would say something.

Dominique sat next to her on the couch. It felt awkward before Dominique spoke.

"I want to apologize for my outburst earlier."

"It's okay. I was just confused because I didn't know if I had done anything wrong."

"No, you didn't. You have been nothing but nice and warm to me since you found me. I was out of line. I shouldn't have snapped, but sometimes my feelings go back to that place, and I get all consumed with them."

"What place?"

"The mental facility. Dr. Jacobs had a tight reign over the women she had working for her. Before she started pimping me out, it didn't feel like a mental hospital. But after she got her claws in us, I truly felt like I was in prison. For some reason, today, when you were asking me all those questions about where I was and saying I needed to check-in, I felt like I used to with her. Although I couldn't maneuver like I was free, I had the autonomy to move around the grounds. She took that from us too. So, I'm sorry. It wasn't you. Please forgive me."

"Oh Dominique, of course, I do. I just never saw you get so upset. But you made some valid points. You are grown, and you have the right to go and come as you please without me all over you. What I'll do is get you a cell. If you do happen to go out, you don't need to tell me where and when you'll be back. Just let me know you're okay."

"No, but I like you want to know when and where. It makes me feel generally loved."

"Well, I'll get the phone, and you'll figure out how much you want me to know. How's that?"

"That's fine."

"Good. So, let's eat."

Nala got up and walked over to the stove and took out the food. Dominique helped her place it on the kitchen table and they sat down. Nala prayed and they began to eat. She wasn't sure if she should bring up what she learned about Lauren Price today. After all, she didn't want to seem as if she was prying again. She decided to let it ride, and she would visit it tomorrow. But Dominique had other plans.

"So, what do you want to know about Lauren?"

Nala nearly choked on her food. She wasn't expecting to hear her mention it. She drank some of her wine and looked at Dominique with surprise. "Huh?"

"Nala, I know you. I know when you got to work the profiler in you looked up her name. You couldn't help it. That's what you do. So, I know you read up on her and that you have a ton of questions, so shoot," she said, eating a carrot.

"Well, I did Google her and was surprised she even existed. I was skeptical if the name and my dream meant anything."

"I can't make you believe. All I know is it's real. When you dream about Robert, it's no dream. He's actually with you. This should have sealed the deal for you."

"As much as I didn't want to believe, I have no choice now."

"So, before I answer any of your questions, I need to say something. Nala, children, adults, or whatever, when they think about their parents they put them in a different light. They don't think about them having sex, being young, possibly getting high at times or whatever the case may be. Those things apply to everyone else's parents but their own.

But parents were young once, and they have a past. Nala, I may not be who you think I am. Yes, I was a high-profile defense attorney who represented the rich and powerful. I looked to have it all, but there was so much more to me. Things you may not find appealing. Do you understand what I'm saying?"

"I think so, but I know you were young once and wasn't always innocent. I'm a big girl; I understand that. I don't see through rose-colored glasses anymore."

"I hope so because if you want to take this walk down Dominique memory lane, it's definitely not for the faint at heart. No judging."

"How could I possibly judge you know you know what I've done. You don't look at me differently. You can tell me anything."

Dominique poured herself and Nala a glass of wine. She sipped some and sat her glass down, looking at Nala. She had shared with her some time ago about the first person she killed when she was a little girl. It was a bully who had been tormenting her for a few school years. Bashing her head in seemed so easy to do, and when she got away with it, she felt invincible. She hadn't realized for some years that the "thing" inside of you that takes you to some dark places can lie dormant for as long as you want *it* to. But *it's* still there. *It* doesn't go away. You just learn to tame *it*. Dominique didn't know where *it* came from. She figured everyone had *it* inside of them. Some people unleash *it,* and others don't.

"I wasn't totally honest with you about Robert and me. We did keep in touch, and we did spend time together after you were born. However, I saw him again, and that's when I learned who he was."

"What do you mean?"

"The first time I saw him after you were born was when you were a month old. However, I saw him again maybe three or four months later. He came to where we lived, or I should say Voorhees? He got a motel room, and you and I stayed with him for a few nights. Then, I stayed with him for a night. Ms. Penelope knew how unhappy I was with your father, so she kept my secret. She didn't know Robert was your dad or who he was, but she did know there was someone. Nala, I loved your dad. I adored him, but he couldn't stay faithful. I hoped after you were born he would change and be the family man I prayed for, but he didn't. Robert came into my life at a time I was broken. I needed something, and he gave it to me. This Ted Bundy-looking white man gave me what I needed," she laughed.

Nala laughed too. She found how Dominique fell for him hard to believe. Robert wasn't an unattractive man, but he didn't seem like her type. Her father, on the other hand, did. He was suave, handsome, and a well dresser. Although he died when Nala was five years old, she still remembers how handsome he was. She remembered how she loved sitting on his lap and rubbing his face. Robert was nothing like her dad in any way. It just goes to show how opposites do attract.

Dominique told Nala how Robert opened up to her. He shared with her how he believed in divine intervention and how he was chosen to begin an extermination of women who sinned. Robert felt like it was his calling after witnessing the things his mother did to his father. He believed God chose him to do His work, and when it was done, he would be rewarded.

"Yeah, I know he felt God told him to kill the seven women. That's what he told me and practically the world."

"I know, but those seven victims were not his first. He killed before then."

"What? Who? How many?

"Three. But I know specifically of Lauren because I helped him."

Nala's heart sank. Her stomach began doing butterfly flips. She tried not to look how she felt, but she was sure her face read it. She couldn't believe how close she and Dominique had become. They didn't just tell beauty secrets; they told secrets that could be damaging if they were revealed. Where did that closeness come from so quickly? Were they truly bonded by the horrors they'd committed? Nala couldn't believe how free they were with one another. She picked up her glass of wine and finished it off. Dominique could tell she was uncomfortable, but this was the walk she wanted to take. There was no turning back.

"How did you help him? What do you mean?"

"Well, Pandora's box is already open, so here goes. When Robert visited us for the second time, he told me about what he had done. The women he murdered. Before he was known for killing the seven women you helped put him away for, he had already killed many years before. I knew of two when he talked to me about Lauren. You see, Robert believed in many things. He truly believed he was chosen by God to rid the world of certain people. I knew it wasn't of God, but he intrigued me so much. By the time he talked to me, he had a plan for killing the seven women, but he said it would be years later when the moon met the sun or some stuff he was talking about."

"But why Lauren? How does she factor into this?" Nala asked, becoming more interested.

"Robert believed in numbers. The seven murders representing the seven deadly sins, and the number three representing the Holy Trinity, The Father, The Son and The Holy Spirit. Before Lauren, he had already killed two women. He needed a third to seal his fate and confirm he was to kill seven women. He asked me did I know of a good girl, a pure girl, who was loved and liked by many and whose death would be monumental. I immediately thought of Lauren; she was all those things."

"So, how did you help him kill her?"

"Well, I didn't physically help him, but I lured her to him."

"How?"

Dominque began by telling Nala how much Lauren respected and idolized her. When she was chosen to work at Dominique's law firm, she was more than ecstatic. Everyone knew how much she enjoyed working there and how blessed she felt to be chosen out of twenty students. Lauren was a hard-working go-getter, and Dominique loved it because it reminded her of her when she was up and coming. The two had not only developed a mentor-mentee relationship, but Lauren considered Dominique a mother figure. At the time of Lauren's death, Dominique's law firm was working on a big case, which Lauren had been very instrumental in helping gather information. When Robert asked of someone he could "sacrifice," Dominique said Lauren but was hesitant. She had really grown to like her, but she was in love with Robert. A broken woman who doesn't feel validated will do anything for acceptance and love. Dominique told Robert about Lauren, and he thought she would be the perfect fit to seal the deal. The plan was for Lauren to meet Robert at a chosen location under the guise of picking up some files, then he would take her. Dominique had to plan it precisely, so it wouldn't trace back to her or the firm, and she did. A few days later, the police were at her law firm asking questions about Lauren and her disappearance. A day later, her body was found.

"Truth be told, that has haunted me for a lot of years. I have deeply regretted luring that girl to her death. She had so much to look forward to in life, and I helped steal it. When you mentioned her name, it was like a flood of emotion overpowered me. I hadn't heard that name in years, and I guess I suppressed it. To me, that was the worst thing I've ever done, and there's no redemption or coming back from that. If I must burn in hell for anything, it will be that," she said with tears in her eyes.

"So, why do you think Randstad revealed it to me?"

"To show you how connected we are. All our hands are dirty with the blood of someone, whether we think they deserved their death or not. We are all forever accountable to the universe. If you never are caught for the crimes you are committing, the universe will punish you. Do you really think Robert's soul is in Heaven?"

"No, I don't," she said with a trembling voice.

"And neither will ours."

Nala thought long and hard about that comment. She did believe in God and thought she had a personal relationship with Him, but, in all honesty, where would she spend eternity based on what she was doing? In her mind, the murders she committed were justified, or so she told herself. At this point, however, it didn't matter. She was past asking for forgiveness. She was in too deep. If she believed God truly loved her and her sins could be washed away, then maybe there was hope for her soul.

"So, they never found out it was Randstad that killed her?"

"No, they didn't. I never heard from him again outside of sending him pictures of you. That was the only contact we had."

"Wow, that's a lot. So, he killed before, huh? So, why do you think it's so easy for us?"

"Why do I think what is so easy?"

"Killing. Why do you think it's so easy? Okay, I know you say that because you and Randstad are my parents that it's in my blood, so to speak. But what about you? I don't think grandmom or grandpop were killers?"

"First of all, who said it was easy? Secondly, I believe, as I have said numerous times, anyone is capable of murder. I believe it's in all of us, but for some, it never is released. For others, like you and me, something triggers it and it awakes. My trigger was the bully. Yours was Kendrick's infidelity."

"Do you think Mom ever..."

"No! She never got bitten by the bug, and thank God. Two murderers in a family are more than enough. I don't know why Robert revealed her to you. But knowing him, it will come out in some way or another. So, there you have it. That's my other dark secret. How do you look at me now?"

"No differently. At the beginning of a new class, I always ask my students if serial killers are born or made? I get an array of answers. Most of the time, it's 50/50. If the tie had to be broken by my answer, I would probably say they are made. I never in my wildest dreams expected to have killed someone, let alone seven people. It amazes me but also creeps me out to think about it. When I transform into that other person, everything I learned and taught has gone out the window. Murder becomes gratifying to me. I wasn't born this way. I was made this way, just like you. I don't look at you differently. I look at you like a human being who has done something that millions of others don't have the guts to do but wish they did, which is murder."

Nala and Dominique sat for a few seconds in deep thought before getting up and cleaning the kitchen. Nala loved the bond they shared, but she also knew it was twisted and sick. A mother and daughter bonded by the murders they've committed isn't usually the thing that connects most mothers and daughters. But they were special, different, and unique. That was her only way to justify their relationship to herself without totally going off the deep end. Nala knew the mother who raised her and who she called Mom with deep love and affection would never be able to understand that part of her, even if she felt she wanted to share it with her. She needed Dominique. She needed her to keep her grounded and sane. She needed her to be her outlet when the nightmares and visions came. She needed Dominique when the beast in her wanted to come out, but she wanted it to rest. Dominque was her doppelganger when it came to murder and keeping her secret.

The more Nala learned about Dominique, the closer she felt to her. It felt good because she had missed over thirty years of a relationship with her. Sometimes, she still felt like that little girl being taken away in the black car, never to see her house or mother again. Nala didn't care what connected them. She was just happy she had her back. After they finished cleaning up and talking some more, Dominique went to her bedroom. Nala sat in the living room with her bottle of wine and a glass. She felt like being mischievous as she dialed Kendrick's number. She knew he would answer, and he did on the second ring.

"I was just thinking about you," he whispered.

"Oh really. Sounds like you can't talk. I'll just...."

"No, no. Give me a sec."

Nala put her hand over her mouth and laughed as she heard Kendrick fumbling around. She could hear Crystal in the background asking who was on the phone and Kendrick responding, Mike. Nala laid back on the couch and thought about asking him to come over. She knew he would come running, but she also knew Crystal would piss a fit. She changed her mind and just decided to have some fun with him.

"I can't really talk right now, but are you okay?"

"Yeah, I'm fine. Did you call the lawyer?" she asked.

"I sure did, and things are cool on my end. I didn't know if you stop divorce proceedings in the middle that you have to pay a fee. I didn't care. I said stop the press!" he said, laughing. "What about you? Did you call your lawyer?"

"Well, not yet. I had some pressing business to take care of when I got home. I'll do it tomorrow."

"I hope so. Oh, listen. What's the deal with your biological mother? How did that happen? I mean, how did you find out? Was it a shock to you?"

"I don't want to talk about that now. I really just called to see if you called the lawyer and to have you tell me something dirty and nasty."

"Okay. Listen. Think about my face buried between your thick, chocolate thighs and me licking and sucking your clit. Think about my tongue playing with your clit as I finger you. Now, think about me sucking you so hard that you grab my head, lock it with your thighs and cum all in my mouth. Can you picture that?"

"Yup, sure can," she said, squirming on the couch.

"Do you want me to come over? Because I can."

"No, not tonight. Another time."

Nala could hear Crystal in the background asking Kendrick something about dinner. He quickly brushed her off. Nala was getting a kick out of the show. She figured that was the scenario a million times with them when he was cheating. Now, she knew what she looked like through Crystal. It was pathetic.

"Okay, I'm going to let you go. The Mrs. calls."

"Don't worry. Before long, it will be me and you again. I'll be back home where I belong."

Nala took the phone from her ear and looked at it with a side-eyed expression. She tried not to laugh into the phone. She didn't want him to hear, but he had no clue he was never coming home. Nala let him continue to tell her all the plans he had before she interrupted him and said goodnight. She could hear Kendrick sounding as if he was going to say, "I love you." Nala quickly ended the call and went upstairs to her bedroom. She laid across her bed and thought about the conversation she and Dominique had earlier in the evening. It was uncanny how much they had in common. The similarities were not what one would expect. Murder was the thing that bonded them. Usually, mothers and daughters are bonded by the clothes they like to wear or the meals they like to cook. This mother and daughter duo was bonded by their body counts.

# Chapter 14

Nala had been up for a while preparing the guest room and house for her parents. She hadn't seen them since she told them her mother was coming to live with her. Although it hadn't been that long ago, she did miss their company and talks. It felt like light years since they were there for a visit because her bond with Dominique grew stronger each day. Every time Nala learned something new about Dominique, the closer she got to her. As much as she didn't want to exclude the woman who raised her, it felt like it could very well happen, and she didn't want it to. She didn't know her fate and the outcome of what she had become and how it would take its toll on the rest of her life. As good as she thought she was, the detectives on the case could be that much better. Although they hadn't proven that yet, many murderers have been caught with the dedication and resilience of good police work. So, whatever time she had remained a free woman, she wanted it spent with loved ones.

The house was smelling of pot roast and potatoes when Dominique went downstairs. Nala had already made coffee and toasted some croissants for breakfast. She sat down as Nala poured her some. For some reason, this morning Dominique looked worried. Her face wasn't as pleasant or reassuring as it had been other mornings. Nala attributed it to her seeing her sister for the first time in over thirty years. So much had taken place in both their lives. Nala thought there was no way Dominique couldn't be nervous. Nala refilled her cup and sat across from her at the kitchen table. She could see Dominique's hand shaking as she scooped a spoonful of sugar and put it in her coffee. Her hands continued to shake as she picked up the creamer, pouring it into her cup. A bit spilled as she became frustrated and wiped it up with her napkin.

"Mom, calm down. What's wrong?" Nala said, reaching over to help her wipe up the creamer.

"Nothing," she snapped.

Dominique buried her face in her hands and sighed loudly, taking a deep breath. She uncovered her face and looked at Nala. It was evident she was scared to death. Nala was nervous about their meeting as well, but she tried not to show it. After all, the two were meeting again for the first time in over thirty years. Would there be any animosity from Dominique to her sister for raising Nala? Or regret? Or jealousy? Nala's mother did have her since she was five years old, so she got to witness all her milestones while Dominique was far away for committing a crime that should have been justified. Nala knew there had to be a million and one emotions running through her mind.

"I'm sorry. I guess it's obvious I'm a little nervous seeing your mother, huh?"

"Yeah, but that's to be expected. I'm sure she's nervous too."

"Why should she be? She had the life I dreamed of. I missed out on raising my one and only child because of a stupid mistake. I can never get those years back."

"Well, I would think she's nervous because she doesn't know how you feel about the job she did in raising me."

"What? I couldn't be anything but grateful and proud. Look at you. Top criminal psychologist, head of the psychology department at your job, author, famous profiler," she said, giggling. "That's one thing my sister doesn't have to worry about is if I think she and her husband did a good job in raising you. They did more than I could ever ask, and I love them both for it."

"I know it would have been the same from you if you were there to raise me."

"Yes, but that wasn't in the cards. Life was the way it was supposed to be. Every long second, minute, hour and day away from you were meant for this time right here. But, I haven't seen your mom in a long time. We were really close, and one day it was all taken away. I'm hoping she isn't disappointed in me."

"No, oh no, she won't be. I promise. She missed you, and the last thing she's thinking about is being disappointed in you. Relax, Mom, okay."

"Okay, I'll try."

Dominique began eating her croissant, but Nala could still see the nervousness on her face. Once her mother arrived and the initial meeting was over, she would be okay. This was long overdue, and Nala was sure everyone was feeling a little on edge. Nala finished her breakfast and started cleaning the kitchen while Dominique got dressed to go for her early morning joggawalk.

As Nala made her way from the kitchen, her cellphone began to vibrate in her pocket. She pulled it out and saw it was a text from Kendrick. She opened it and it read, "Good morning beautiful. Just thinking about you." Nala saved it in her archives and headed upstairs. She bounced on the bed and pulled up her lawyer's phone number. She dialed the number and laid back. Nala was told her lawyer was in court and wouldn't return to the office for a few hours, so Nala left the message for the secretary. However, she knew he would return her call to get the story firsthand. In Kendrick's mind, he stopped the divorce proceedings permanently, but Nala was just postponing it for a while.

***

When Nala heard the doorbell ring, her heart dropped. Dominique stood up and smoothed out her dress as if she was awaiting her prom date. They both looked at one another and smiled. Nala opened the door and rushed to give her parents a big hug. Her mother stumbled back from the hearty greeting.

"Oh, it's so good to see you, Mom and Dad. Come in."

"It's good to see you too," they said as they walked in and put their bags down.

As Josephine raised up from putting her bag down, she locked eyes with Dominique's. The tears welled up in both of their eyes as they stood for a second looking at one another. Anxiety had gotten the best of them as they breathed heavily from the excitement. They looked at one another carefully and slowly up and down as they walked toward one another. Josephine reached her hand out and delicately touched Dominique's face. She caught the tear that had managed to escape her eyes.

Josephine lowered her head, took both of Dominique's hands, and placed them in hers. She rubbed her hand across each finger as if ensuring they were all there. The tears began to flow down each of their faces as they could no longer hold them back. Josephine opened her arms, and Dominique fell in them like a long, lost child. The gut-wrenching cries that came from them swallowed the big house. Nala's father put his arm around her shoulder as they both cried.

"I missed you so much," Josephine said with her voice cracking.

"And I missed you as much, too," Dominque replied.

The two continued to hug as Nala's dad walked over and hugged them both. The moment was very emotional as Nala stood back, watched and cried. After what seemed like forever, they let go of each other and began to laugh while they wiped the flowing tears from their faces with their hands.

"You're looking good, Firestorm," Nala's dad said with a smile.

"Firestorm?" Nala asked with an inquisitive tone.

Nala's dad turned to her and shook his head, laughing. She felt a story coming on as she leaned against the table in the hallway with her arms crossed. Dominique and Josephine had put their arms around each other's shoulders and stood waiting for what Lawrence had to say.

"Well, this here woman, your mother, was as spunky as they come. She was sweet and all, but if you crossed her, she was a fireball. She lit up a few people with her words. No one wanted to cross her if they could help it." He smiled.

"Yeah, I can see her being that way," Nala said. "Well, come on. Let's go in the family room and sit and talk."

Nala led the way as they followed behind her. She had set up some snacks in the family room to eat until it was time for dinner. Dominique and Josephine sat next to each other and couldn't help touching one another. It was almost as if they were trying to see if the other one was real. Nala felt like they both had a heavy weight lifted from them. After many years, the initial shock of seeing one another was over, so now they could relax and get to know each other once again. Nala poured everyone a small glass of wine to soothe their anxiety. They all sipped it slowly, but Nala drank hers down in one gulp. She poured herself another one and smiled. They all raised their glasses and smiled back.

"So, sis, how have you been," asked Dominique.

"Blessed. Life has been good to me."

"It looks like it has been. I want to finally say in person that I am so thankful and truly humbled for the job you and Lawrence did in raising Nala. She is such a beautiful young woman, and that is all due to you two. I love you both so very much for that. I can never thank you enough."

"It was already planted when we got her. You did that," Josephine said, sniffing.

"Yeah, you did, Firestorm. We just finished what you started. But now you're home, and you can try and make up for some missed time. It's so damn good to see you, girl," Lawrence said with tears flowing down his face.

Dominique got up and walked over to Lawrence. He stood up, and the two hugged again. Nala knew the reunion would be emotional, but she wanted to lighten the mood and fill it with laughter.

"Okay. I know there must be some stories associated with this nickname Firestorm. Do tell," she said, clapping her hands.

Dominique and Lawrence began to laugh as they stopped hugging and went to sit back down. That was the mood Nala wanted, happiness and laughter. She figured tears would flow again, but, for now, she wanted to see her parents smile. Nala couldn't wait to hear what stories they had hidden to share. She knew a side of Dominique that was fire, but she wanted to know the side they thought was hot. They all sat looking like the statue of the thinker. Nala couldn't wait to hear what stories lie beneath. Suddenly, her dad perked up and lit up like a Christmas tree. He began to smile and shake his head.

"We had gone to your mother's law firm for a black-tie event. This was before she met your dad. He was tight on your momma. He wanted Ms. Dominique, and we all knew it. But your mom at the time wasn't interested..."

"Or she was playing hard to get," interjected Nala.

"Who knows. But your father was after your mother that night something fierce. Finally, being sick of him, she turns around and says, 'Are you really that desperate, or do I just turn you on that much?' Your father was shocked that every woman there was after him, and your mother was the only one..."

"Playing hard to get," Nala said again, laughing.

"No, I wasn't playing hard to get. It was just that he kept sniffing around me like a dog."

"And she told him that too," laughed Lawrence.

They talked about more good times as they ate dinner and drank wine. It felt good to finally have them all in one place enjoying themselves. With all that Nala had done, a normal evening was definitely food for the soul. After dinner, they went into the family room for coffee and dessert. They talked for hours and laughed just as long. As Nala sat back on the couch observing all the happy flow, a text message came through on her cell phone. She picked it up, and it was from Kendrick. She was curious to see what he had to say as she opened it. She was surprised to see it was a video of him masturbating and talking about what he wanted to do to her. Nala laughed out as she looked at her parents, who were engrossed in their conversation. She got up, slipped out of the family room, and went into her office. Nala turned the volume up more on the phone and watched the video several times. As much as she didn't want to admit it, it was turning her on. Nala dialed his number, and he quickly answered.

"Hey beautiful," he seductively said.

"Seems like you have a lot of time on your hands, among other things."

"This is what you do to me. You've always done this for me, no one else, Nala."

"Really? So why did you cheat?

Nala could hear Kendrick's heart beating through the phone. She had asked that question before and never felt like she got the right answer. But was there a right answer? Was there an explanation as to why her husband cheated three times, of which she knew about? If he loved her as much as he professed, why did he fuck other women? Nala didn't want to believe it was because he didn't love her, but she wanted to hear his justification. What could he say that would make breaking her heart okay?

"It had nothing to do with you. It was me."

"And what was you? What made you have sex with three different women and get one pregnant?"

"I don't know. Maybe I needed to feel like I was the shit. I mean, being married to Dr. Nala Jordan, top criminal psychologist and profiler, can be very intimidating."

"So, what you're saying is you needed someone to stroke your ego? I thought I did that. I never made you feel

184

like you had to live in my shadow. I always wanted you to be a part of whatever I was a part of, and I thought you were."

"And I was. Nala, it's just sometimes I felt like it was Dr. Jordan and her husband. Sometimes, I felt like a sidekick."

"How could you have felt that way? You're accomplished in your own right. You were never in my shadow. So, why didn't you ever say anything? I honestly thought we were happy. How naïve of me, huh?"

"You weren't naïve, and it was never anything you did or didn't do. A man couldn't ask for no better woman than you. You're beautiful, sexy, smart, and intelligent. It was all me, my stupidity, my weakness, my ego. Baby, I want to make it up to you. Please give me a chance? I promise I will never hurt you again."

"But you're willing to never hurt me in the process of hurting Crystal. How's that going to work for you?"

"I love you Nala, that's all I know. If I have another chance to make it right with you, someone may have to get hurt. That's life, right?"

Nala looked at the phone and smirked. It didn't surprise her that Kendrick was willing to throw Crystal under the bus for what he wanted. Although she couldn't stand Crystal and could care less what happened to her, this is what men do when they are finished with you. Men were just a means to an end in her book. Loyalty and honesty weren't words some of them knew or lived by. There was a time Nala would have done anything for Kendrick. He was her world, her life. The first infidelity hurt her, but she figured he's going through something, he'll bounce back. The second infidelity cut her deeply, but the love was still there.

But this one, this one here. Kendrick not only cheated on her again, but everyone knew about it but her. How degrading to be at work and everyone else knows your husband is screwing his secretary. Then, to make matters worse, he gets her pregnant. Dealing with infidelity is one thing, but being reminded of it daily is insane.

"Yeah, I guess. Hey, let me ask you something. You know I've been helping with the serial killer case in Philly. What do you think about that?"

"Hmmm, well, I think it's deep. I don't think anyone should die because they stepped out on their marriage. Is cheating wrong? Yes. But is killing someone right for cheating? Nope."

"Well, I don't know if I agree. Sometimes, people have to learn the hard way."

"With their life? What are they learning if they're dead? Nothing. What do you think? I mean, do you honestly think it's cool to kill someone for cheating?"

"I sure do think it's okay. Eye for an eye. My pain for your life."

Nala could feel the chill in Kendrick's silence. She wanted him close but not too comfortable with her. She didn't think he would believe she could kill anyone. In his book, that was not his Nala. Maybe another scorned woman, but not Nala. She smiled devilishly on the other end as she waited for his response. What would he say?

"Really? Wow. I didn't think you would feel that way. Interesting. Anyway, I was hoping to see you. The text I sent was a taste of what I want to do to you. Can I come over?"

"It's not a good time. My parents are here. It's family time, you know."

"Well, what if I come and get you, and we take a ride somewhere?"

"No, I'm just going to stick around here and take care of some things. So, the baby shower is coming up, huh?"

"Yeah, next week."

"Nice. Is she excited?"

"Uh, yeah," he nervously answered.

"Hmmm."

Nala could hear Crystal in the background asking Kendrick who he was talking to. Of course, he lied, and she didn't pursue any more questions. Before she disappeared into the night, she asked for a foot and back rub, and Kendrick nonchalantly answered, okay.

"I have to go anyway," Nala said.

"I can't wait to be back in my house, my bed, in you. Damn girl, I miss you so much."

"Down, boy. Patience. I'll talk to you soon."

"Okay. Love you, and you don't have to say it back. I just need to say it, and I need you to hear it."

"Cool. Good night."

"Good night, Beloved."

Nala sat at her computer and began scrolling through her messages. She came across the invitation for the baby shower, but this time it was accompanied by the list of attendees and those who hadn't replied yet. The invitation had an urgent message stating the deadline to reply had passed, but the address was provided if people wanted to send a gift. Nala sat back in her chair and picked up her glass of wine. She drank some and sat the glass down on her desk. A smile came over her face as she got lost in her thoughts.

Crystal's baby shower would be one she definitely would remember.

***

Kendrick laid back on the bed with a smile on his face and his eyes closed. All he could think about was Nala and being back with her. Crystal had walked into the bedroom and looked at him. He hadn't even noticed she was there. She felt sick to her stomach, not because of the pregnancy but because of Kendrick's distance. As much as she wanted to believe he was excited about the baby, it just didn't show. She felt, at times, she had to force him just to give her a kiss goodbye when he left for work. Crystal felt like she was losing him, and she hated that feeling. She didn't want this relationship to end the way all the others had. She would fall in love hard, be their eye candy for a while, then she would get dumped. As much as she didn't want to face it, her mother was right. Crystal was too old to believe a baby could keep a man around, but she prayed this one would. She put her hand over her belly and rubbed it gently. Her little angel would be here soon, and she hoped things would change. Maybe when Kendrick saw the baby, he would fall in love all over again. That was her prayer. If it didn't happen that way, she was out of options.

Crystal took a deep sigh and walked over to the bed. She sat next to Kendrick as he opened his eyes. She smiled at him as he gave her a phony one back. Crystal felt like she was about to burst into tears, but she held her composure. She was tired of him seeing her cry.

"What's up?" he asked nonchalantly.

"Nothing much. I thought you might want to hear the changes I made for the baby shower."

"Do I need to? That's more your thing than mine."

"Huh? It's our baby. I thought that meant something."

"You know I didn't mean it like that. I meant it's more a girl thing than a guy thing."

"Well, I said we could have a unisex shower, and you said no. I thought that would have been so cool. How come you don't want to have your friends come?"

Kendrick sat up in bed and folded his arms. He looked at Crystal like he was the principal scolding her for running in the hallway. He hated to be so blunt with her, but at times he felt like she liked it when he was that way. Kendrick didn't know how much longer he could fake not being in love with Nala and calling off the divorce. All he could think about was going home to her, and Crystal was putting a damper on his feelings. He told himself he didn't have much longer before the baby was born, then he could really land it on her.

"Crystal, I'm still a married man. My friends and co-workers were at my wedding. They love Nala. Yes, we aren't together, but there're still people who think this is wrong. To be honest, if I had invited them, they wouldn't have come. I didn't want to put you in that predicament."

"So, remind me to not put their names on the invitation list for the wedding since I'm not good enough!" she angrily said.

"Yo, slow down with that wedding stuff. I keep telling you to take one step at a time. Let the baby be born first, then we'll see about the wedding."

189

"What? So how long do you think I'm supposed to stay engaged? I'm not going to be engaged for years playing house."

Kendrick grunted and got up from the bed. She could hear him mumbling and grumbling to himself as he gathered some paperwork and left the room. Crystal got up and followed him as they went down the stairs. She was breathing heavily from being angry and tired. Kendrick sat on his leather recliner in the living room and began looking over the paperwork in his hand. Crystal stood in front of him with her hand on her hip.

"What?" Kendrick asked, looking up at her.

"Do you love me?"

"Man, come on with that, Crystal. Why does everything have to go back to whether or not I love you?"

"Because it does. That's the basis for everything. Whether you love me or not. So, do you love me?"

"Yes, Crystal, I love you.

"Are you in love with me?" she asked as her voice trembled.

"That's real important to you, isn't it? If I'm in love with you or not."

"Well, shouldn't it be? We're about to have a baby. We're engaged. I would think being in love would be something of major importance. It's not to you?"

"Crystal, I'm not trying to be baited into where you're trying to reel me. I have some papers to grade, so let me get to it. We'll talk later."

"The question is simple and only requires a yes or no answer. Are you in love with me?"

"No, Crystal. I'm not in love with you."

Crystal looked at Kendrick and felt like her entire world had just crumbled. She had no doubt that somehow Nala was involved, inadvertently or advertently. Crystal felt like her legs were about to give out as she turned to walk away. The tears began to flow heavily down her face while she made her way up the stairs to her bedroom. She hoped he would run after her and tell her how much he loved her, needed her and wanted her. She hoped he would say, 'let's get married today and throw caution to the wind.' But he wouldn't, and he didn't. That only happened in romance novels, fairytales and movies. This wasn't a Harlequin romance, or a fairytale, or a movie. It was her life. The same life that always dealt her this hand.  Her fate was to have a baby and be without its father. Her fate was to once again be alone.

## Chapter 15

Nala was feeling pretty good when she got to work that Monday morning. Her weekend with her parents was more than she could have hoped for. They decided they would have an adult sleepover once a month until they felt like they had enough of each other. From where Nala sat, that would be no time soon.

Nala sat behind her desk with her hot cup of coffee going through her emails. She hadn't heard anything from Detective Chase in quite some time, so she was surprised to receive an email from him. She picked up her coffee and sipped it. The hotness of the liquid felt good going down her throat. Nala opened his email and read it over. "Hmmm," she said as she sipped more of her coffee. Nala hadn't killed anyone in quite some time. She didn't know if she was like her dad and the urge was gone after so many kills or if she was going through a cooling-down period. She still hated Kendrick, and she still hated married cheating men, but the urge to kill them wasn't as profound as before. Detective Chase had informed her that since the case was going cold, they had to remove the manpower they had working on it. It was assigned to several seasoned detectives who would still investigate. Detective Chase was hell-bent on catching whoever killed another cop, but they had to move on. He thanked her for her service and wished her well. Nala sat back in the chair with a smile. Had she gotten away with killing seven men? Was she going to go down in history as a female serial killer who was never caught? She remembered Randstad telling her she would be as notorious as Bundy,

Gacy and Dahmer, but she didn't believe him. From the looks of things, his premonition may have been on point. At this point, all Nala wanted to do was make Kendrick suffer. For some women, being cheated on meant you cry, feel like shit, feel as if your world has crumbled, and your life is over. For Nala, it meant hurting the man terribly who hurt her and hurting other men who hurt their woman. It may seem farfetched and overboard, but, from her lineage, solving problems or being vindicated by someone who hurt them meant destroying them. Nala got up and picked up her coffee and briefcase and headed to her class. She set her things down on the table and scooted herself upon it. She crossed her legs and rocked them back and forth. Her students prepared themselves for class as they removed their laptops and other information needed from their bags. Nala looked at Jessica and saw something in her that made her want to tell her some things. She didn't know why she felt a connection to her, but she did. Nala knew Jessica worshipped her and would probably do anything for her. Whatever the case, Nala could breathe a little easier with Detective Chase and the Philadelphia Police Department taking a step back on the case.

"Good morning to my future profilers. I am so eager to hear what you have come up with on your prospective cases. I know you have worked hard, independently I might add, and I am very proud of you. You know, being a profiler means you have to become intimately close to your cases. It's like dating. It's the first initial impression, then you add in some time as you're getting to know that special person, and if things work out, he or she is the one. Profiling a case is no different. I know you have spent countless hours gathering information, speaking to people and going over and over and over the information provided. Hopefully, you have developed some relationships that may be beneficial to you when you graduate. So, having said that, let's hear from Jessica."

"Well, I had the case of the female serial killer in Philadelphia who still hasn't been caught. I worked closely with Detective Chase to follow up on leads, interview people, and go over the crime scenes. At times, it felt like we had a big break, one we could use to catch this person, but then it would be nothing. I must admit it became frustrating at times because I know this person is catchable."

"How do you know that?"

"Because everyone makes mistakes, even the ones who think they're the best at what they do. You see, right now, this woman is thinking to herself, 'I got away with killing seven men.' However, in actuality, she hasn't. Just because someone hasn't been caught yet doesn't mean they got away with it."

Nala giggled and asked, "Doesn't it mean just that? That they got away with it? After all, they haven't been caught, soooo it's safe to say they're home free."

"Oh no, I beg to differ, Dr. Jordan. Not being caught yet just means you're still being pursued. Eventually, they'll have to pay the piper. All I'm saying is she shouldn't get too cocky or too comfortable."

"Hmmm, okay. So, what was the outcome of your investigation?"

"Well, the PPD had an entire unit devoted to this case. They even petitioned the help of the famous criminal psychologist, Dr. Jordan," Jessica said, smiling. "But as we all know, manpower equates to money, and it was just costing them too much money to keep all the detectives and cops they had working the case. So, they downsized their manpower to two detectives and closed the unit."

"Things like that often happen when the case becomes cold, or there aren't enough viable leads to keep the case open with a significant amount of manpower working it. As Jessica stated, I was called in as a consultant on the case to do the profiling. Sometimes, we don't get our perp, regardless of the best intentions and detectives working it. So, what we do is move onto the next in hopes we'll get better results. Thank you, Jessica."

Jessica nodded her head, and Nala moved onto the next student. Although Jessica thought she shouldn't get too comfortable with not being caught, Nala felt like she had the upper hand. For the moment, she would revel in it.

After class was done, Nala began packing up her bag. She noticed Jessica moving slowly as if she was waiting for the rest of the students to leave to be alone with Nala. Once the room was cleared, Jessica walked over to Nala and stood in front of her. Nala was curious to hear what was on her mind.

"Yes, Jessica. What can I do for you?"

"Do you really think Lady Ice is uncatchable?"

"No, I don't believe that. I think anyone can be caught. However, sometimes the universe just doesn't align with that, and sometimes people get away with murder. I mean, look at Jack the Ripper. Never caught. The Black Dalia murderer, never caught. I could go on and on," Nala said, grabbing her bag and walking out the door.

"That's true, but it seems to me like she's killing out of hurt and revenge, so she's running on emotions. That makes me think she's going to slip up," Jessica said, following her down the hall.

"She very well may slip up, but who knows? All you can do is your best and move on like I said in class." Nala stopped at the entrance to her department.

"I just want to..."

"Catch her? You just want that one defining moment that may define your career? You want to be like Clarise Starling and catch Buffalo Bill, so those lambs will stop crying? You will get your chance, trust me. You haven't even finished school yet. Give it time. You'll get your shot."

"I'm not trying to become famous, Dr. Jordan. I just want to help catch a killer."

"You're not trying to become famous?" Nala laughed. "We all want to be famous, whether they know who we are or not. Listen, you've done a wonderful job in both my classes. I know you will do well in your career. Don't rush it. Enjoy this downtime because this job can be very dark and lonely. Enjoy your friends while you can. Enjoy your man while you can. Enjoy all that is good while you can. Do you understand what I'm saying?"

"Yes, I understand."

"Okay. So, we have a few more weeks of class, and then it's a wrap. I look forward to reading your entire report. Have a good day, Jessica."

"You too."

Nala turned around to enter her department and was shocked to see Crystal waiting for her. Nala thought to herself that Kendrick must have really let her have it since he thinks they're getting back together. Crystal had her head down and hadn't noticed Nala walk up. When she noticed someone in front of her, she lifted her head and looked as if she had been crying. Nala felt nothing for her. She didn't care if she had been crying or screaming or whatever. Everything happening to her was karma, and that made Nala happy.

"Forgive me if I didn't respond to your invitation to your baby shower. I have a root canal scheduled for that day," Nala said sarcastically. "And furthermore, don't you have a restraining order against me? Where is your third party?"

"Oh, fuck the restraining order! All I came here to ask is how did you do it?"

"My secretary is my witness that you came here hostile and cursing me. And did what? What are you talking about?" Nala said, unlocking her office door and going inside. Crystal angrily followed behind her.

"How did you get Kendrick to think you want to be with him?"

"Umm, I've never been pregnant before, but I did hear women go through an awful lot of emotional swings. Is this one of yours because I have no clue what you're talking about?"

"Oh really? Kendrick has been so distant and cold towards me for a while now. That can only mean you're involved somehow."

Nala laughed as she sat behind her desk and Crystal stood. How pathetic was she? This wasn't the first time she had gone to Nala when she felt threatened that Kendrick didn't want her anymore. She was the type of woman that thought her looks would get her by all her life. She never thought that once the sex and thrill were gone a man wanted a woman with substance, intelligence. Sadly, she had neither.

"So, let me get this straight. Because you feel Kendrick doesn't want you anymore, it has something to do with me? Is that about right?"

"Yeah."

"Girl, please. I don't want Kendrick. I bailed that ship a long time ago. You're barking up the wrong tree. Maybe he's doing to you what he did to me. Stepping out."

"No, I don't think so. It's you. Just admit it! You hoed your way back into his life somehow. You can't stand the fact that I'm pregnant and we're engaged."

"Lord help her." Nala laughed. "If you were so secure in your pregnancy and engagement to Kendrick, I wouldn't even be a factor. You wouldn't even be worrying about me. If Kendrick doesn't want you anymore, it's because for once in his life he's come to his senses. He knows you aren't mommy material or wifey material. He lost all hopes of that when I left him. So, I don't know what to tell you, other than what goes around comes around. Now, I need you to leave my office before this turns really ugly. And if you don't, I'll call the cops and have your ass locked up. How'd you like that?"

Crystal walked to the door and turned around to look at Nala. As much as Nala tried to act as if she still had the upper hand, Crystal knew with her pregnancy came some leverage to Kendrick in her life. As long as there was a baby, there was Kendrick, despite if they married or not. For that, she took comfort.

"Well, Nala, the invitation still stands to my baby shower. You're welcomed to come. After all, that may be the closest to having a baby you'll ever get."

Nala chuckled as Crystal walked out of the office. She thought to herself that was what desperation looked like. Nala packed up her briefcase and grabbed her pocketbook. She put on her coat and left her office, locking the door behind her. When she got to her car, she dialed Kendrick's number and waited for him to answer.

"Well, isn't this a surprise? I was just thinking about you," Kendrick said.

"Oh really? I guess your woman was thinking about me too because she just left my office."

"What?! Why?"

"I don't know Kendrick, you tell me."

"I don't know why she… oh, wait a minute. I know why she probably came to see you. See, yesterday she asked if I was in love with her and I told her no. Maybe she thinks you're the reason behind that, which in all honesty, you are."

"So, you don't know how to play it cool for a while? I don't need that bitch coming over to my office. It doesn't look good. Now, I need you to be cool until things are a go."

"And, when will things be a go? I told my lawyer to call off the divorce proceedings, and so did you. Why can't we be together."

"Soon, okay, soon. I have some things on my end to tie up first. Just be patient."

"Well, when can I see you again? I miss you. Damn girl, I miss you a lot, if you know what I mean."

"I don't know. I'll call you." Nala hung up the phone to Kendrick, saying something she didn't hear. She hoped her tattling would cause more trouble between them.

*** 

Dominique was cooking dinner when Nala got home. She could smell the fried chicken and yams when she entered the house. Nala was surprised. This was the first time since her mother had been with her when she cooked such a big meal. She had made breakfast every now and then, but nothing of this magnitude. Maybe it was all due to her seeing her sister after thirty-plus years. Nala walked into the kitchen, and the table was covered with food. There was a coconut cake, macaroni and cheese, stuffing, cabbage and blueberry muffins. Nala was flabbergasted as she sat down and watched her mother remove the remaining chicken from the deep fryer.

"Are you hungry?" she asked.

"Wha-wha, what is all this?" Nala asked with a big smile.

"I just felt like cooking today. I feel really, really good for the first time in a long time."

"I'm glad, Mom. This looks so good."

"Well, I haven't cooked in years, so let's hope it taste as good as it looks."

"I'm sure it will."

Dominique sat across from Nala and reached for her hands. She held them as she prayed. Nala could tell how happy her mother was. She had a glow about her, and it made Nala so delighted. Because something so dark as murder was what linked them, times like the past weekend with her parents and dinner today made life seem normal. Dominique finished praying, and they began fixing their plate. Nala tasted the macaroni and cheese first and felt like it was a piece of heaven on earth.

"Mmmm, Mom, this is sooo good!"

"When you were young, that was your favorite dish. We had it every Sunday for dinner and during the week, maybe once or twice. If you had it your way, we would have had it every day. You used to love helping me make it. Most of the time, you would try to eat all the cheese. I miss those days. That's another reason I wanted to cook for you today."

"Well, my taste buds say thank you."

"So, how was your day?"

Nala smiled as she continued to eat her food. She was smiling because the food was good, and she was smiling because of her visit from Crystal. Her mother could tell she had some news to share as she poured them each a glass of red wine. Nala didn't care what it looked like as she drank it down in one gulp. Her mother simply poured her another glass and continued to eat.

"Well, I had a visitor today at my office. Crystal."

"Interesting. Why?"

"She seems to think I'm the reason why Kendrick doesn't want her anymore."

"Are you?"

"I may be, but that's not my problem."

"You're right, and she should feel threatened and uncomfortable. Like I told you before, they need to know you're here. They should never forget who you are and what they have done to you. She should be scared when she wakes up in the morning until she goes to bed at night. That's the fear you should be imposing on her. You understand?"

"Yes, Mom, I do."

"Before I uh, killed your father, there was no warning. I stayed in my private pain and heartache and suffered. It all came to a boiling point when I went to his house that night. Had I fucked with them for a while, that may have been enough for me to get over it."

"But fucking with them, as you say, wasn't enough because I killed seven men."

"Killing is in your blood; it's in your DNA. I think you would have eventually gotten the bug whether Kendrick did what he did or not."

"Hmmm, you think?"

Nala and Dominique finished their dinner and conversation before going into the living room with their wine. Dominique sat on the recliner and let it back while Nala sat on the sofa with her feet crossed. Her conversation with Jessica came back to her as she sipped her drink. She felt like if Jessica could take over the case and pursue it independently, she would. Nala had never shared everything with her mother about the murders, only vague things. For some reason, she was feeling even more connected to her and wanted her to know everything.

"I'll be right back," Nala said as she went upstairs to her bedroom. When she returned, she had a red metal box in her hand. Dominique curiously looked at her as Nala sat back down. "Come sit next to me, Mom," she asked as she crossed her feet again on the couch.

Dominique got up and went to sit next to Nala. Dominique could tell she was a little nervous from the way she was breathing and holding the box. Her chest heaved up and down slowly as the sound of her breathing filled their space.

"Whatever it is, baby, you can tell me."

"The first time I killed, I felt like my life was truly in danger. I didn't set out to do that, but I did. The second time I killed, I wanted to. It gave me power, a rush. From then on, I was unstoppable. I remember each one of them, what they were wearing, what they smelled like and how their touch felt. I was repulsed. However, I needed something to remind me that I was actually there, and I was responsible for their deaths, so I took things from them that obviously didn't mean anything to them."

Dominique watched as Nala slowly unlocked the metal box and opened it up. She wasn't shocked to see what was inside. What would have shocked her was if Nala hadn't kept anything. Nala had shared a lot with her mother. After all, her mother knew she was the Lady Ice killer who had murdered married men in Philadelphia. If you could share that type of information with your mom, nothing else seemed shocking or off-limits. Dominique looked in the box and then at Nala. She was waiting to hear what she had to say.

"My first prey wasn't meant to be one, but he got the ball rolling, so to speak. Darryl Jones was his name. Married man from West Oak Lane who thought he could beat the sex out of me. I really went to his house to just unwind and get myself together before driving home. I was a little tipsy. However, he had other plans. So, I had to defend myself. After I killed him, I took his watch because his time was up," she said, pulling the gold watch out and handing it to her mother.

"Rick Taylor, my second prey. Mr. Suave, Mr. The Shit. Handsome but definitely a dog. I almost ripped his penis straight from his body. I took this from his wrist," she said, pulling out a gold link bracelet from her box.

"This little beauty of a money gold clip belonged to Lincoln Phillips, my third prey."

Dominique sat watching Nala attentively as she held each item in her hand. As she spoke of each victim, it was as if she was gaining immense pleasure thinking of them. Dominique believed the pleasure came from remembering the murder as opposed to the victim.

"These gold cufflinks showed how much money my fourth prey, Mr. Preston Jacobs from Chicago, had. I'm sure he was banking being an architect."

"If it was at all possible, my fifth prey, Lieutenant Raymond Friscoe, was by far the worse. He was the biggest piece of shit there was. While his wife was dying of lupus, Mr. Policeman was out screwing everything that would open their legs for him. He didn't deserve his wedding ring or badge, so I took them both," she said, handing them to her mother.

"Next, there was Calvin Watson. Sadly, he didn't get much airtime in the news. The police were already swamped with five unsolved murders before him, so his death just was clumped in with the rest. He pissed me off too. So much so, I decided to take his ring finger all together," she said, lifting a small glass bottle filled with clear liquid and his finger.

"And last but not least, Bryce Wilkins. A true dog. He came on to me while he was celebrating his wedding anniversary with his wife upstairs waiting for him to return from the bathroom."

"So, Mommy, do you think I'm deranged yet?" Nala said, taking the mementos and putting them back in the metal box.

Dominique looked at her and smiled. She thought to herself, *how could I think my baby girl is deranged?*

Nala wasn't crazy. She was highly intelligent and incredibly smart. She wasn't by far deranged. She was just walking in her destiny she and Robert had created. A destiny filled with murder, unstableness, and no regrets. If Dominique thought her baby was deranged, then she would have to think that of herself, and she didn't.

"No, baby, I don't think you're deranged. I just want to know. Are you done?"

"Done? Nala asked.

"Yes. I know you feel like killing these men is vindication for what Kendrick did to you, but sweetie, they're not Kendrick."

"I know, Mom. But just for those few minutes it takes to snuff the life out of them, they are Kendrick."

Nala stood up with the metal box in her hand and looked at her mother. She smiled and left the room.

## Chapter 16

Crystal was excited about her baby shower today, although Kendrick was still distant emotionally. She could sense he tried to be supportive, but it seemed hard for him to do. She felt as if she had enough to deal with today, so she let him have his feelings. However, she hoped that once the festivities began, he would lighten up and be there for her, even if it was a lie. She needed him to be there for her in front of her friends and mother, despite where he probably really wanted to be, which was with Nala.

Crystal's baby shower planner had really done a wonderful job of bringing her wishes to life. The small, quaint hall looked amazing with its Disney princess theme. The guests were starting to arrive as Crystal grew anxious and happier about the day. Kendrick stood off in the background watching as the people filtered in. Crystal stood at the entrance with her stomach protruding through her dress and welcomed them. Kendrick couldn't believe he was having a baby with her. Their rolls in the hay were never meant to get to this. Pregnant, engaged and living together. Kendrick always wanted this with his wife, not the side piece. He chuckled as he thought about how he wouldn't be in that predicament if he had strapped up.

The little hall was almost filled to capacity as Crystal's mother walked over to him. She tried not to look disgusted, but she wasn't good at not wearing her emotions on her face. Kendrick took a deep breath as he tried to act as if he didn't see her coming. Whatever she had to say, he wasn't interested. She stood next to him with a drink in her hand

and a forced smile on her face. Crystal glanced at them and smiled.

"Are you going to at least act like you want to be here?" she asked.

"I'm here, aren't I? So, I must want to be."

"Well, it would be nice if you showed it by supporting my daughter. Why aren't you over there with her greeting the guests?" she asked through clenched teeth and a false smile.

"Your daughter is fine. She doesn't need me. When it starts, I'll join her."

Crystal's mother took a sip of her wine and chuckled. She despised Kendrick. All the late-night phone calls from her daughter crying within the last few months made her want to hurt him. However, she knew the outcome would be the same as it always is. She hated that Crystal never listened to her when she tried to tell her not to get involved with married men. The result would always be the same, which was Crystal getting hurt. At least before she could dust herself off and move on, but this time she had a baby who would forever remind her of her indiscretions.

"You know, you make me sick. I tried to tell Crystal to leave you alone, but she was too far gone, too quickly. You have done nothing but hurt my baby and use her. It wasn't enough that you were cheating on your wife with my daughter, but you had to go and make her believe you wanted more. Moving in with her, proposing to her and getting her pregnant. Where does that happen in the player manual? I mean, do you think it's okay to hurt people the way you have? My daughter and your wife?"

"Oh, please, Ms. Carter. Don't act as if you care anything about my wife. As far as Crystal is concerned, I didn't sign up for this, but it's here, and there's nothing I can do. I'm going to take care of my daughter and not just financially. But me and Crystal, we're done. She knows that."

"Boyyyy, I'd sure hate to be you when the wrath comes down. Maybe it's good my daughter and granddaughter won't be around because I don't want them in the path of destruction."

She walked away and joined her daughter as the last of the guests arrived. Crystal gave Kendrick a look, which meant it was time for him to act like he wanted to be there. He walked over to her and hugged her around the waist. The photographer began taking pictures as everyone smiled and began taking pictures with their cellphones. Afterward, the two sat at the table for two and began to watch the slide show. The pictures were mainly of Crystal's pregnancy, doctor's appointments and just candid shots. A few showed a once happy couple before Nala came back on the scene.

The baby shower was going better than Crystal had expected. It was everything she dreamed of and more. She especially loved the poster size picture of her and Kendrick. He held her naked stomach looking down at her as she looked up at him. The photographer had captured how she felt in one shot. She had her man and was about to have his baby. What more could she want? After the meal, the planner announced they would play a few games before opening the gifts. Crystal laughed while the women played a game where they had to measure her stomach with toilet paper they had previously torn off. The toilet paper that measured her perfectly would win. There were a few more games of guessing how many miniature baby bottles were in the big container, which foods did she crave the most during pregnancy and the dirty diaper game.

When they were done, the planner led Crystal and Kendrick to two gold throne chairs. They sat down, and she placed a crown on her head. It was time to open the gifts. The planner began to hand Crystal the gifts as she opened one, then Kendrick. The cameras flashed while Crystal held up clothes, packages of pampers and other things she could lift. Kendrick held the boxes that were heavy such as the crib and changing table. The room was filled with gifts as they had to move some in the hallway because it was becoming crowded. Crystal was extremely happy, and for a moment, so was Kendrick. As they finished opening the gifts, there was one left, a DVD.

"I was told by my wonderful planner there is one gift left. It's a video from my university family with well wishes. Before we watch it, I would like to thank each of you for making this day so special. Kendrick and I are just so happy for all the gifts, well wishes, thoughts and prayers given to us. We are both excited about our little princess's arrival. We can't wait to hold her and love on her. Before we watch the video, I want to say to my planner, my friend, Camille, thank you for a wonderful day. The food, the decorations, the games and music were all so wonderful. You did a fantastic job, and I love you and thank you from the bottom of my heart."

"You're welcome. It was my pleasure. So, as Crystal said, this is the last gift. It was requested to be shown at the end. So, without further ado, let's watch."

The video began to play within five minutes of Camille returning from the tech booth. Camille had instructed the tech guy to start the video at that time. Everyone looked anxiously at the screen as there was music playing in the background. Crystal looked at Kendrick and smiled. She took his hand in hers, and they both watched the screen. Within a few minutes, the sounds of moaning were heard. The guests looked around, confused as the sounds filled the small room. Kendrick released Crystal's hand as he sat on the edge of the chair. Crystal began to breathe heavily as she tried to figure out what was going on. Suddenly, the image of Nala and Kendrick was on the screen. Kendrick stood up in shock as everyone gasped. The images flashed of them having sex in the living room, the car, and in their old bedroom. He couldn't believe Nala had taped them and sent it to Crystal.

"Oh, my God! Turn it off," someone yelled.

Camille ran out of the room as Crystal's mother ran over to her. She was crying hysterically as Kendrick ran out of the room to follow Camille.

"Mmmm, yes Kendrick, yes! Who do you love, baby?"

"You baby. Always you."

"You miss me? You want me back?"

"Yeah, baby. Damn girl, this shit is good."

"Fuck me, Kendrick!"

It seemed like eternity plus forever before the DVD was turned off. The guests gasped and shook their heads as they looked at Crystal. No one knew what to say, but their angry and sad facial expressions showed it. They felt so sorry for Crystal as her mother hugged her trying to console her. Camille had returned, and it was evident she was crying. She walked over to Crystal and rubbed her back. "I'm so sorry. I didn't know," she said.

Crystal's mother shook her head to Camille, letting her know they didn't blame her. The guests didn't know what to do. Should they leave? Should they stay? Should someone whip Kendrick's ass? Kendrick had returned to the room, and all eyes burned on him. Crystal walked over to him and spit in his face. He wiped it with his hand and just stood looking at her. She was still crying hysterically.

"How could you do this to me? Why?" she yelled.

"I didn't mean for this to happen, but you knew the deal."

"What?" her mother yelled as she charged toward Kendrick and pushed him with all her might. He fell against the table, knocking it over as some of the guests stood up and grabbed her. She tried to get away from them as Kendrick stood with a smirk on his face smoothing his shirt.

"I swear you better get out of here before I kill your sorry ass."

"I got to get out of here! I got to go!" Crystal yelled as she grabbed her coat and pocketbook. Camille tried to stop her, but Crystal was as strong as an ox.

"Crystal, where are you going? You can't drive!" Camille pleaded.

"Please, I gotta get out of here," she yelled, running out the building and getting into her car.

Kendrick grabbed his jacket and headed to his car. Once inside, he immediately called Nala. She knew what the call was probably about, so she didn't answer. She sat on the couch with a bottle of red wine and a glass, laughing as he repeatedly called her. Kendrick sat in the parking lot and watched as some of the guests began to leave. The women looked like cackling hens as their mouths moved quickly. Their hands made gestures, and their heads bobbed side to side. He knew the conversations were about how he was a low life, a dirty motherfucker, a scumbag and if he had done it to them, how he would be dead. Kendrick laughed at them. In his book, more than likely, their man was cheating on them. He thought to himself how many of them secretly know their man is a cheater but stay anyway. Although they were upset and saddened by what happened to Crystal, they were also relieved their secret was still locked in the closet, maintaining their ability to be judgmental.

Kendrick started the car and pulled out the driveway to head to Nala's. As low as it was, the secret was out. He didn't have to hide anymore. He tried Nala again but still no answer. His heart raced in anticipation of seeing her. If everything went the way he wanted, he would be back home in his bed tonight.

When Kendrick pulled up to Nala's place, he looked at his phone because it had been blowing up the entire ride. It was Crystal's mom, and he definitely didn't want to speak to her. He heard enough of what she had to say earlier, and that was enough. He was glad he wouldn't have to be bothered with her anymore because she was a piece of work. Kendrick got out of the car and knocked on the door. He stood there for a second and knocked again. Nala stood behind the door smiling as she heard him mumbling some words. He knocked several more times, each time getting louder as if that would make whoever was inside open the door. Nala sipped on her wine and stood there until the knocking stopped. She could hear him walk away and get in the car. Kendrick looked at his phone again, and there were six more missed calls from Crystal's mother and just as many voicemails. Instead of calling her back, he retrieved the first message.

"Where the hell are you? Crystal's been in an accident! You need to get to Jefferson Hospital!" she yelled.

Kendrick decided to listen to the rest of the voicemails to see if they explained why she was in the hospital, but they didn't. She just yelled frantically while crying and telling him to get to the hospital. Kendrick figured this was it. She went into labor, and she was having the baby. Before he pulled off, he tried Nala's phone once more and still there was no answer.

Kendrick arrived at the hospital and went into the main entrance. He asked for the labor and delivery floor and went upstairs. A little excitement filled him as he thought about seeing his baby girl. He hoped she was okay from the accident. When the elevator doors opened, he expected to see Crystal's mother and a few friends waiting in the lobby area, but there was no one there. He looked around before walking to the nurse's station.

"Uh, excuse me. My name is Kendrick Jordan, and I believe my fiancée is here. Her name is Crystal Carter."

"Okay, sir let me check," said the nurse, typing on her computer. "Oh, I'm sorry, but we have no one here by that name."

"Are you sure? Her mother called me like twenty times telling me to get to the hospital because she was having the baby."

"Let me check again." She went through her computer once more. "No, sir, I'm sorry. What is her name again?"

"Crystal Carter."

The nurse began typing something on her computer and looking at the screen. She picked up the phone and called someone, asking if they had a patient named Crystal Carter. Kendrick was visibly worried as he looked on anxiously. The nurse hung up the phone, and despite her trying not to look concerned, she did.

"Mr. Jordan, your fiancée is in emergency."

"Emergency? Why? Is there something wrong with the baby? Was the accident that bad?"

"Sir, I have no details for you. However, if you go through that long hallway and take the D elevator, it will direct you to the emergency room."

Kendrick darted down the hallway and took the D elevator as told. When he got to the emergency room, he ran over to the nurse's station and leaned against the desk. He was breathing heavily as he tried to gain his composure.

"Crystal Carter. Is she here?"

The nurse typed in her name and asked, "Are you family?"

"Yes. I'm her fiancée and baby daddy. Is she here?' he asked angrily.

"One second, please."

The nurse phoned someone in the back and spoke softly. Kendrick could hear her telling someone his name and saying he was the fiancée. Kendrick was growing angrier by the second because he had no clue what was going on. Why was the nurse so secretive? As he stood waiting for some answers, a doctor appeared from the double doors. Kendrick got a knot in his throat and felt like he was going to vomit. Something was wrong. He could feel it. The doctor looked at

Kendrick then the nurse. She shook her head, and he walked over to him.

"Uh, excuse me. Mr. Jordan."

"Yes. Where is my fiancée? Is the baby okay?"

"Sir, there was an accident. A terrible one. I'm so sorry to have to tell you this, but your fiancée and daughter succumbed to their injuries. "

Kendrick felt like the room had begun to spin. He could see the doctor's mouth moving, but no words were coming out. The room slowly stopped spinning, but everything was moving in slow motion. He felt like he was dreaming.

"Succumb," he said softly. "What do you mean, succumb?"

"Sir, they're gone. I'm so sorry." The doctor tried to put his hand on Kendrick's shoulder, but he pushed it away.

"Succumb! They're gone! What do you mean? What do you mean?" he yelled.

"Sir, please. I know this is hard. Do you want to sit down?"

"Fuck no, I don't want to sit down! Where is my family?"

Kendrick pushed the doctor to the side and ran through the double doors. He yanked back each curtain, hoping to see Crystal and his baby possibly banged up some but alive. The patients and nurses in the emergency room were startled as he ran, calling out Crystal's name. From one of the rooms, he could see Crystal's mother appear. Kendrick stopped and stood there. The security guard ran behind him and took him by the arm. Crystal's mother walked slowly toward him. Her eyes were swollen, and tears were pouring down her face. Kendrick stood there as the security guard held his arm. The doctor walked over to him and whispered he could let him go. Kendrick's heart raced as Crystal's mother reached him. He knew the worse had happened. His baby and Crystal were gone. He tried to move, but his body felt like a ton of cement. Without warning, Crystal's mother punched him in the face. Kendrick fell back and hit the floor.

"You killed my babies! You killed my babies!" she yelled as the security guard pulled her away.

Kendrick wiped the blood from his lip and stood up. He stumbled into the nurse's station as he tried to gain his composure. As he stood straight up, he saw a few of Crystal's friends run out of the room toward her mother. The security guard led her through another set of double doors. She screamed and kicked as she tried to get away but couldn't.

"Mr. Jordan. If you would like to see your family, please come with me," the doctor said.

Kendrick walked a few steps and stopped. He looked at the doctor as his legs gave way. He fell to the floor on his hands and knees and began crying. The doctor kneeled, trying to help him up. The nurses all looked on, feeling overwhelming sadness. One of them walked over and helped him to stand. Kendrick stood and began walking toward the room with the doctor. When he got there, he started to hyperventilate.

"Breathe, Mr. Jordan. Slowly," the doctor instructed.

He began to feel his breathing return normal as he stood there. He slowly pushed the door open and walked inside. Crystal was lying on the table. She was covered in a white sheet up to her neck. Beside her bed was one of the hospital baby cribs. He could see a small baby inside who was also covered up to her neck. Kendrick walked over to the bed and looked down at Crystal. He could tell they tried to clean her up as much as possible, but the gash over her right eye and scrapes to her face were still prevalent. Kendrick stood and looked at her, feeling an enormous amount of guilt. Tears began to well in his eyes again as they fell rapidly down his face.

"I'm so sorry." He whispered, kneeling to kiss her on the forehead. He walked over to the crib and looked at his daughter. Even in death, she was beautiful. Kendrick reached in and picked her up. Her little body was cold as he covered her with the sheet. Kendrick walked slowly to the chair in the room and sat down. His angel was beautiful. She had a head full of black straight hair. Kendrick opened the sheet and began counting her fingers and toes. She had them all. He smiled and covered her back up. The tears wouldn't stop falling as they dropped on the sheet making little wet spots. "I'm so sorry, sweetie. I'm so sorry," he cried.

Kendrick held his daughter close to him before getting up and returning her to the crib. He never wanted any of this to happen. As much as he wanted to be back with Nala, he didn't want it that way. Kendrick tore a paper towel from the dispenser and wiped his face. He walked over to Crystal once more and looked at her. No matter what, she didn't deserve this.

He kneeled once more and kissed her. "Bye, baby. I love you." Kendrick turned and walked out of the room. It was as if he was a movie star by the way everyone looked at him. The doctor walked over to him and patted him on the shoulder.

"I'm very sorry for your loss. Is someone here with you? Will you be okay driving?"

"Yes, I'll be fine. What happens now?"

"Well, the mother doesn't want an autopsy, so the bodies will be taken to the funeral home of her choice. I, uh, I don't know the history of your relationship with the mother, and right now, emotions are at an all-time high. However, at some point, you two need to get together to discuss the arrangements and to be a support for one another."

"I don't think that's going to happen. Look, I have to go."

"Be well. Take care."

Kendrick shook the doctor's hand and walked out of the emergency room. When he reached his car, he got inside and began to cry again. His heart was broken. As sad as he was, anger began to creep up. Whatever fight there was between him, Nala and Crystal, his daughter was no part of it. She didn't deserve that fate. Kendrick dialed Nala's number again, and she still hadn't answered. He started the car and began his drive to Nala's house. This time he wasn't leaving until he saw her.

\*\*\*

Kendrick pulled in front of Nala's once more and got out of the car. This time, instead of knocking on the door, he was banging and yelling her name. Within a few seconds, Dominique opened the door. She could tell Kendrick was quite angry. She looked at him with cynicism as Kendrick tried to hold back the tears that were welling in his eyes.

Whatever brought him to her daughter's door looking defeated, angry and sad, it was Karma.

"I need to see Nala."

"Sure, one minute," she said, trying to close the door.

"No, don't close the door. I need to see Nala," he said, brushing past her and going into the house.

"Now, wait just a minute. You don't have a right to barge in here like that. Get out!"

"No! Nala, where are you? I need to see you! Now!" Kendrick yelled, walking into the living room. "I know you're here! I need to see you!"

"I'm calling the police," Dominique said, reaching for the phone.

Nala appeared and took it from her hand. She walked into the family room where he was shouting and stood in the entrance with her arms folded. "Here I am, Kendrick. What do you want?"

"Why would you do something like that? Why would you send that to her?"

"Oh, I see you guys got my gift. How was the baby shower? Did you like my gift?" She laughed.

"What? Did I like your gift? That shit wasn't cool."

"Oh well. Life ain't cool sometimes. Get over it. That little bitch swore she had the upper hand. Now, I bet she is crying her heart out, asking herself, 'why he do this to me?' Karma bitch, karma."

"She's not asking herself anything, Nala, because they're dead! Crystal and my baby! They're dead!"

"Dead? Hmmm. Really?"

"So, now what? What do we do now? How are we supposed to go on together? How do you expect me to get past this?"

"How did they die?" she calmly asked.

"Car accident. After watching the video, she ran out of the baby shower and drove off in her car. I don't know all the logistics, but they're dead."

"Karma. Didn't want to hurt the baby, but sometimes war has innocent casualties."

Kendrick backed up and looked at Nala. After all she had done, he still loved and wanted to be with her. The pain of losing his child would take some time to get over, but he knew it would get easier. He needed Nala right then, even if she was cold and bitter. She was all he had left.

"War? Casualties? Look, I know you didn't mean for this to happen. Right? I mean, you aren't that cold-blooded, right? I guess with time, we can get through this. I'll just need you to be patient with me."

Nala laughed out loud and shook her head at Kendrick. She couldn't believe him. It always boiled down to what Kendrick wanted and what Kendrick needed. He didn't care about anyone but himself.

"Patient with you? Your baby and fiancée are dead, and all you can think about is being with me? You are so pathetic! Get the hell out of my house! I don't want you! I never wanted your trifling ass back! I'm still filing for divorce. I already called my lawyer to tell him to continue with the proceedings. You're just a sad son of a bitch, and I got you! I finally got you!"

"What? Look, we can get through this. I just need time! Please, Nala, don't do this to me now! I know you didn't mean to hurt the baby! I know you still love me! Dammit, Nala, don't fuckin do this! I gave up everything for you! For us!"

"It was never about me, but always about you! Hell, it wasn't ever about Crystal or the baby either! Everything is always about Kendrick and what he wants. Well, how does it feel to have nothing? Now is the best time to show you how it feels to have your heart ripped out by someone you love. Now is the best time to show you how it feels to love someone and think they love you back, but they don't. Now, Kendrick, is the best time to say, fuck you and go to hell!"

Nala walked to the front door and opened it. Kendrick began yelling and screaming, knocking things off the fireplace. Nala ran upstairs. When she returned, she had a 45-caliber gun in her hand. Kendrick had managed to cause a mess in the family room, but he hadn't broken anything. Nala stood at the entrance and pointed the gun at him. "If you don't get out of my house, I'll kill you. And please know it wouldn't be hard to do."

"You bitch! You set this whole thing up! You were never going to get back with me!"

"By George, I think he's got it!" She laughed. "I wanted to hit you where it hurt, and it hurts, doesn't it? Just leave Kendrick. Have some type of dignity, will you?"

Kendrick slowly walked to the door, with Nala still pointing the gun at him. Dominique stood to the side, watching. She really saw for the first time how deep Nala was in the abyss. Dominique didn't know if she could come back from it.

"Don't come back here. Don't call me. Don't say my name because I'll feel it. Just forget me."

"You hate me that much, Nala? All because I cheated on you? I made a mistake! People cheat all the time, but they don't do what you did!"

"You're right. Sometimes, they do worse. And yes, Kendrick, I hate you that much!"

Kendrick walked to the door and turned around. He stood there looking at Nala and did not recognize her. She was not the woman he had fallen in love with. She was not the woman he wanted to have children with. And she was not the woman he hoped to grow old with. She was a stranger, and hating her wouldn't be hard. His heart was beginning to harden, and soon there would be nothing there for her.

"Karma Nala, remember that. Karma."

"Thanks for the tip." She slammed the door.

"Are you done now?" asked Dominique.

"Yeah, I'm done. Now, we need a vacation!"

# Chapter 17

Nala and Dominique sat on the beach in Jamaica drinking an island drink. The sun was blaring down on their skin as the waves in the ocean looked to be playing with one another. It was a serene place, and they both needed it. Despite her demands to Kendrick to not call her, he hadn't listened. He called at least three times a day and texted just as much. Supposedly, he had time to think, and he wasn't angry with her anymore. He understood why she did what she did, and he was sorry for it. Nala didn't care what type of revelation he had come to. She was done with him and wanted him to be done with her.

Nala and her mother sipped on the fruity drink that had a kick to it. She could feel herself getting tipsy, and rightfully so since she was on her third drink. Nala looked through her black sunglasses at all the handsome men walking the beach. She wondered how many were on vacation with their mistresses. She wondered how many wives were in the dark about their husband's extra-curricular activities. Nala finished up the drink and gestured for the waiter. He was a tall, dark, well-built man with swimming trunks full of thick manhood.

"Can I have another?" she seductively asked.

"You sure can. And you?" he asked Dominique.

"No, thank you."

"I'll return in a sec," he said with a deep baritone voice.

He turned and walked away, and Nala looked at his rock-solid ass and huge thighs and thought about how she could wrap her legs around him. She fanned herself at the thought.

"So, is she asleep?" asked Dominique.

"For now."

"You have to ensure she stays asleep. Waking her for your own personal gain and desires will make you lose yourself. You don't want to do that."

"Mom, I'm not the same, Nala. She died a long time ago. That woman who believed in love, in marriage, in commitment, honesty, trust, yadda, yadda, yadda is dead. This is the new me. The new me who takes risks and eliminates threats."

"Are you sure you like her?"

"No, Mom, I love her."

"Okayyyy. Please, just don't lose yourself. Anyway, I'm glad you did come to your senses and went to your father's lawyer to get what he left. Never, ever, turn down money, especially a lot of it." She grinned.

"Yeah, well, I figured my bank account wasn't suffering but adding a cool million to it didn't hurt either."

"You got that right!"

The waiter brought the drink back and sat it down next to Nala. He gave her a smile showing his perfect white teeth, and walked away. Nala thought to herself that before leaving the island, she would let him taste her. She deserved it. Nala sipped her drink and looked out to the ocean. She was in a good place. Detective Chase had emailed her a few days ago to tell her there still were no leads, but the case remained open. In her book, she had gotten away with murder. Just like her father years ago, she felt she had rid the world of scum, cheating, and married men. What good were they? All they did was cause pain and heartache in the wives who believed and trusted them. She knew the death of their husbands was hard in the beginning, but if they honestly looked at it, they were better off without them.

"I love you, Nala. Just be sure when you unlock that box and wake her again that you can come back from it."

"I hear you, Mom, I do. And I understand. All I know is that the woman inside me who allowed me to do the things I did will always be a part of me. She is going nowhere. She is a part of me. She is me, and I absolutely fuckin' love her."

"Okay, okay. Let's enjoy this sun and view."

Nala smiled, and the two tapped their glasses together and drank their drinks. Nala didn't know where life was taking her, but she was up for the ride. For the first time in a long time, she felt like she could breathe. As she sipped her drink, she noticed a man walking toward them. She looked over her sunglasses at the dark, chocolate man walking her way. He kneeled next to her and smiled. Nala could feel her pussy throbbing and getting wet. He was more gorgeous than the waiter. Dominique closed her eyes and smiled.

"How you doing? I'm Mark."

"Hi Mark, I'm Nala."

"So, what brings you two lovely women to Jamaica?"

"Sunshine and relaxation," she said.

"Well, you'll definitely get that. But what about some fun?"

"Yeah, that too. Why, you looking to have some fun?" she asked, looking at his wedding finger.

"Oh yes, and there's nothing like fun with a couple of beautiful women," he said.

"Oh, no dear, just one woman. I'm good right where I am," said Dominique.

"I understand," he said, smiling.

"So, Mark, I see you're married. Where's your wife?"

Mark smiled and looked down at his ring. He looked busted, as if he forgot to take it off. He knew he couldn't lie about being married, so he just hoped Nala would go along with him.

"Oh yeah, well, yes I'm married, but I'm here alone, on business. You know what they say. What happens in Jamaica stays in Jamaica."

"I thought that was Vegas."

"It's Jamaica too." He laughed.

Nala tried to tame the beast inside of her that was fighting to get out. It would be so easy to kill him, but she wasn't there for that. She really wanted to enjoy herself and relax. However, bad habits die hard. She took him by the hand and reached over close to his face.

"You sure you ready for me? I bite."

"I hope so."

"Okay, Mark, let the games begin," she said with a smile.

**Book 4 of the Lady Ice Series is**

**Available Now!**

***Darkness has engulfed the small town of Crescent Ville, VA.***

Criminal psychologist Dr. Jessica Newsome learned everything she knows from Lady Ice herself. She grew up in Crescent Ville and vowed to never return after the disappearance of her mother. However, her once beloved town now holds the secrets to five murders and the mystery of her mother's disappearance. Local man Tony Cox has confessed to the murders, but there are no bodies. He will only reveal the horrific details to Jessica. She doesn't want to return home, but she must determine if Tony's secrets run deeper than just the recent murders.

Read Book 4 Now

www.ingramcontent.com/pod-product-compliance
Lightning Source LLC
Chambersburg PA
CBHW060323260626
47160CB00007B/2665